OLIVER IREDALE

MY IMPURE
BLOOD

COPYRIGHT

For Mum.

My dedicated reader, carer and warrior.

Couldn't have done this without you.

CONTENTS

PROLOGUE

Heed my plea Goddess, I, Maria Darby, reject you, Thomas Blake.

Rain bounces off the pavement, soaking me to the bone. Shivering, I rush up the stoop and pound on the door. As I wait, I catch my breath. I ran miles to get here. Jacob is my only hope. If he refuses, I shudder to think what could happen. My hands go to my stomach, the bump barely noticeable, yet I can hear my child's heart. If I strain my hearing.

I shouldn't have waited so long to tell Thomas. Nevertheless, that wouldn't have changed anything. He's a blood purist.

That thing inside you is an abomination! A disgusting aversion to nature.

Locking the memory away, I wonder how Thomas could despise, and be repulsed at the idea of our child? I can't understand.

I've known that I wanted children my whole life, and the moment I met him three years ago, on my twenty-second birthday, I couldn't wait to conceive ours.

You are beautiful, Maria. I'll never harm you.

He broke that promise, he has hurt me so deeply – hurt us. Why wouldn't he want a mini us? Wiping my tears away, I pound on the door again, pure terror bubbling in my stomach – what if Thomas dared to follow me?

I'll always find you.

I can remember our early days very well; we were two individuals who should hate each other. For I am a delta werewolf, while he is a vampire and leader of a clan. No one would have imagined us to be the perfect match, though we were, and I love Thomas dearly, despite breaking our soul bond.

Sighing, hate blooms in my heart.

It must be terminated, Maria!

Why didn't I take heed of those disgusted by half-bloods? I should have considered if Thomas was one of them. My love blinded me, and my child will pay the price.

I will not be its father!

Will my child hate me, because their father will not consider them his own?

Thomas hadn't even known I had taken a potion of fertility. And I know he won't change his mind about this, he's always been stubborn. I wish I could be safe in my pack; however, I know I won't be. Especially after what happened to my sister's human mate – it was no accident. I can still see the look on Hannah's face. *Logan... he's dead.*

The door finally swings open. Jacob stands there, an elderly white-haired man with strange eyes – a sign he's a magic user – white irises, brown horizontal pupils, and the whites of his eyes, the sclera, are black. He ushers me inside silently as I explain everything that has happened. He has to help, Jacob was the warlock I bought the fertility potion from, he has to...

By the end of explaining, I'm sobbing uncontrollably on his sofa in the living room. Jacob does a peculiar thing; he agrees to help. For free. The solution is easily enough solved. The ritual of secrecy.

Once the ritual is completed, no supernatural creature will ever find, see or touch us. Jacob being the sole exception, as he is the caster. Though there is a limit. Once a magic user dies, any spells they cast are undone. So, there is a time limit of safety.

"The ritual won't harm my baby, will it?" I worry aloud.

"No," Jacob assures. "Except, there may be consequences."

"What type of consequences?"

"Unknown, your child was conceived through magical means, who knows what this ritual will do to him."

"Him? It's a boy? How can you tell, I'm only two months pregnant?"

Jacob smiles knowingly, his hand going to my shoulder. "I have a talent when it comes to predicting certain things."

"I'll have a sweet little boy." I grin, stroking my small bump. "I already know his name. It shall be Clay; it was my grandpa's name."

"It is a lovely choice."

I stand, and Jacob starts banishing the furniture in his living room, so he can set up the ritual. Once it is ready, he makes me lie down in the centre. Slicing his hand with a knife, he starts chanting, and I sense the magic pooling into me, filling me. We're going to make it, Clay, you're going to survive, we're—

Snapping back to present, I shake my head, wondering why my mind drifted to that day...

Continuing my dressing into my favourite long-sleeved blue dress. I ponder what to do today. I have the day off from the hospital.

I find it hard to believe that everything I was remembering happened over sixteen years ago.

It must be terminated, Maria!

Shivering at the memory, I push it away. My sweet little boy is practically all grown up. Sometimes I miss my family and even Thomas. I seldom talk about them or the supernatural. What point is there in talking about it? We live as humans.

Oxstead is the town we settled in, somewhere in Hampshire. It is an average little town. A good place where I raised my son. Jacob set me up here, then we lost contact. I have a quick smoke out of the window. Smoking calms me, a habit I struggled to avoid during my pregnancy. I reflect on that night; the warning Jacob gave me. The ritual did indeed have an effect on my sweet boy. His eyes are cursed or something, as whenever someone looks directly into them, they see their death. I can't count how many times I've seen my own demise. I have not told him that his eyes are probably the way they are because of the ritual. Possibly a bad parenting move.

Sighing dejectedly, I crush the stub of my cigarette into the ashtray, shut the window and head downstairs. Clay, my sweet boy, is sitting on the kitchen table, sucking on a blood bag. His caramel hair, which he inherited from Thomas, is pulled back into a man-bun. The dark clothing, he wears highlights his inhumanly white skin, and he has his silver-mirrored aviator sunglasses on, that I gave him a handful of years ago.

I can remember when he was around four, Clay asked me, *Mummy, what am I?* I told him honestly, and over the years, I've tried to make sure he doesn't feel like an abomination. But there is only so much I can do; I can't lie about how most view hybrids – as abominations.

It must be terminated, Maria!

"Morning," he mumbles glumly.

I roll my eyes inwardly; a solemn heartbroken teenager who thinks I don't know he was dating Sabrina Green. He deserves better. She barely gave Clay the time of day.

"Morning," I reply. "Slept well?"

"Fine."

I snort, such a talkative fellow. Clay pushes his sunglasses up his face, they had slipped down a bit, and for a split second I saw his eyes.

Goosebumps crawl over my body, flashes of my death entering my mind. I'm being held down, and Thomas is hitting me.

You are beautiful, Maria. I'll never harm you.

I've seen that moment many times. He lied. The doorbell rings. I groan and trudge out of the kitchen and into the hall, Clay following, probably hoping it's that Sabrina girl.

Opening the door, I freeze, my whole world is shattered into millions of pieces. On the other side of the door is Thomas. Jacob is dead, that is the sole way he could have found us. Could today be the day I die?

You are beautiful, Maria. I'll never harm you.

Liar! This is it; I know it, I can feel it in my gut.

Thomas hasn't aged a day, unlike me, a woman now of forty-one. Goddess, he's still dressed in a twentieth century three-piece suit, well-maintained Oxfords and bowler hat, like usual.

"Father," I hear Clay mumble, Thomas tries to move past me, I block him and I stifle a growl when I spot the others. He brought his clan.

"You should have not been born," Thomas snarls at our son, and my heart shatters.

"Please, Thomas," I beg, "he is our son."

"He's no son of mine."

He pushes past, strutting towards my boy, my Clay, my world. No. He will survive, I promised that to myself all those years ago. I lunge at Thomas, throwing him through the wall and into the kitchen.

"Run, my sweet boy, run!" I scream as I fight my ex-mate and his clan of vampires.

Shamefully, they subdue me quickly. I pray to the Goddess that I bought Clay enough time.

Thomas victoriously hovers over my kneeling form, a viscous smile on his handsome face, as he begins punching me.

You are beautiful, Maria. I'll never harm you.

Liar, liar pants on fire. I have seen this so many times, when I looked into my sweet boy's eyes. I do not fear death. I know my fate is sealed – that I will die – and I have no regrets. Clay was all I ever wanted.

Darkness begins to ebb into my vision, the claws of death sinking deep into me. I don't know if I was the best parent. There were parts in his childhood that I'm sure I failed my sweet boy. My wolf surges inside me, and I feel the familiar sensation of trying to shift into my wolf form.

I hope Clay knows that I loved him, that he was my world. That I will not stop looking over him from the afterlife. Goddess, please allow him to have a great life. No, let him live an amazing life. My sweet boy deserves it. I sink into oblivion, my pain and consciousness evaporating.

CHAPTER I

I have to move on, I've slept in the abandoned warehouse for too many days. Plus, the location is compromised, as a bunch of homeless teenagers broke in and robbed me of my cash last night. Of course, I woke when they broke in – I'm a light sleeper – but I could tell they needed it more, so I let them take it. Though, if someone had tried to take my bag, I would have snapped into action.

Licking my lips, I realise I'm ravenous and parched. I need warm food, water and blood. First thing, first – money.

I survey possible marks from the passage of foot traffic flowing by. No one pays me a second glance. So many people – all from different walks of life – I search for the perfect one.

Finally, the Goddess smiles down upon me as I spot him. A businessman in an expensive suit, on his phone. He's a clueless idiot. Bumping into him, I easily slip his watch off his wrist – an expensive little accessory. Greg's pawnshop, here I come.

Trekking a few blocks, I enter the familiar pawnshop: *Own It, Sell It, Buy It.*

Greg is a stout, bald, sixty-year-old man. He sits behind the counter on a hard wooden chair, filing his nails. The pawnshop's small space is well utilised, full of knick-knacks, jewellery and electronics. Soundlessly, I toss the expensive watch on the counter.

Greg huffs, discards his file and examines my bounty. "Ten pounds," he grunts, pulling a crinkled note from the cash register and hands it to me. I don't bother arguing, Greg knows I steal what I sell him. I should be glad he isn't a snitch. Departing *Own It, Sell It, Buy It*, I cross the street and enter a cafe. The café doesn't serve any warm food. Not that I could afford something decent with my ten-pound note.

I swallow my emotions; the cashier is nervously eyeing me like I could infect him with my poverty. Sighing internally, I pay and collect my three cheese sandwiches and two bottles of water. My stomach grumbles as I meander over to a booth and shred the plastic covering my food.

The café has four booths, as the sole seating area, hardwood flooring, pink painted walls, a counter with a cash register, and their refreshments are displayed opposite the entrance. The single visible employee stands behind the counter, the other two employees are in the back room. Unscrewing one of the water bottle lids, I take a deep long swig. Water eases the craving for blood, and bottled water is nice for once, instead of rainwater.

Sighing bitterly, I dwell on my life. It feels longer than two years that I've been homeless. It is hard living on my own on the streets, running and hiding.

You should have not been born.

Those were the first words my father spoke to me, and I hate him so much. Why did he have to be a pureblood extremist? I'm thankful Mum chose me over him. I'm not sure why, how could she forsake her soulmate for me?

By choosing me, I got sixteen years of mundane bliss. Thanks to a spell, a warlock cast that made it impossible to find us through the use of magical or non-magical means. Nevertheless, it came to an end when the warlock died. The ritual he performed on Mum and me was undone upon his death.

Unaware the warlock had died, we were unprepared when Father arrived with his clan. We were no match. Mum was just a Delta werewolf with rusty fighting skills, and I was too scared to be any help. I was a coward, and when Mum shouted, *Run, my sweet boy, run,* I obeyed. I regret that.

Over the years, Father and his clan have got close to me on occasions, resulting in a few showdowns. The good news about my hybrid status is I'm faster and stronger than them. And many of Father's clansmen aren't daywalkers, just him and a few others. I wonder why some vampires can walk in the sun and others can't. I guess that's one of life's mysteries.

The café's bell chimes, as somebody comes through the door, a beautiful teenage girl. She's roughly my age with extremely tanned skin, and she possesses dark brown eyes that seem ancient. Her hair is shoulder-length, midnight black, and she wears a yellow tank top, a leather jacket and leggings that hug her slim curvy figure.

She strides confidently over and sits opposite me. Something about her is unnerving, taking a sniff I realise why: werewolf.

"Is my father hiring werewolves to do his dirty work again?" I enquire, trying to sound calm. "Has he really sunk that low once more?"

She laughs, it sounds musical, except it lacks emotion. "I don't work for Thomas Blake." Her accent is a combination of English and American. "I've come to help you – I'm Melody Morning."

"Clay Knight," I reply. "I suppose you know that."

"Yes, and I know you don't believe me when I say I wish to help you."

"No one helps someone out of the kindness of their heart."

"No," Melody agrees. "I simply wish to offer you – my protection."

I almost cackle at her offer. I doubt she could keep me safe. Plus, the last time I trusted someone to help me – I almost got my head ripped off my shoulders. I won't go into another Johnny situation.

"Do you think my offer is amusing?"

"Yes," I deadpan.

She quirks an eyebrow. There is an air of indifference about her, as if she doesn't care about me. Then, if that were true, why offer her help?

"You can't help me. Only I can help myself."

"True words. Sadly, you won't. You will die in three days. A fixed point without my help."

I snort and thrust my right palm forwards. "Really, don't you need to read my palm to see the future?"

"No, I see the future perfectly fine without your palm."

"I don't believe you."

"I know, you don't. You lived a human existence, aware of magic and creatures like you and I, though never talking to anyone else. Save for your mother, who didn't like to speak about that stuff. So, ask a question, ask me how I can see the future?"

"Okay, I'll bite. How can you see the future?" I gasp as her eyes flash luminous silver. "Mum told me about the four types of werewolves: Delta, Gamma, Alpha and Omega. So why did she not mention a werewolf like you, with silver eyes? Is it genetic?"

Melody seems to consider the question, giving me time to remember the details Mum told me about her kind. The most common are Delta werewolves, like her, their secondary werewolf eyes are orange, and in a pack, they work either in subservient roles or become pack warriors. Gamma werewolves are more dominant, their secondary werewolf eyes are purple, and they have strong protective instincts and are normally pack warriors, or given the coveted role of the Beta in a pack, which is the second-in-command. Alpha werewolves are the most dominant and strongest. Their secondary werewolf eyes are red, and they can only be the Alpha of the pack, or the heir to a pack, as Alpha's are born leaders, not followers. Omega werewolves have a submissive nature and are normally given subservient roles. It would be unlikely to see one as a pack warrior, and their secondary werewolf eyes are yellow.

Finally, Melody speaks, choosing her words carefully. "No, what I am isn't genetic, and your mum didn't mention my kind because we are unique, some believe us a myth." She takes a deep breath before continuing, "I am a sacred werewolf, blessed by the Goddess. She chooses a few and grants them with a certain gift. Mine is the ability to see the future, past and present. I aptly call it the Sight, and because of it, I know you will die in three days if you continue on alone. Near the London Eye, I believe."

"You're crazy or a fraud or—"

"Telling the truth," Melody interrupts, rolling her eyes. "I could be telling the truth that I'm a seer. Do you really want to die in three days, alone, or do you want to come with me and risk it all on the chance that I might save you, and give you a better life?"

"Are you hitting on me?"

"No, I'm trying to help you." She rolls her eyes again. "Only I can help you. Let me help you."

My throat aches, and I look down at the table to see I have devoured my sandwiches and already drained a water bottle. They have not sated the thirst – I need blood. It has been two days, and if I go any longer, I will go into a blood frenzy. And tonight, it is predicted to rain, meaning I need shelter. Curse my need to be warm, why couldn't I be cold-blooded?

"*If*. I'm not saying I trust you or that I will stay with you – as I've been surviving fine on my own – nevertheless, if you take me somewhere warm where I can rest, and get someone I can drink from, then I'll come with you. Not because I think I'm dying in three days – because you are obviously crazy."

She sighs dejectedly. "I'm not crazy. In three days without my help, you will die."

"Good thing I'm taking you up on your offer then, crazy girl."

"For blood and a hotel room, not my protection."

"Are you sure you aren't hitting on me?"

She wrinkles her nose. "I'm sure. Now come on, we best be moving. Your father is closing in on our location. And just so you know, I already have a hotel room."

"What!" I exclaim. How could she mention my father so casually? Then go straight onto talking about hotel rooms?

Melody doesn't respond, she simply gets out of the booth and exits the café. Scowling, I follow her into the warm day.

CHAPTER II

A taxi is waiting to take us to the hotel. Neither of us speak the entire hour-long journey. I wasn't expecting much, maybe I should have, as it turned out to be an expensive establishment. Upon entering, the hotel's employees sneered at me, disgusted by my smell and appearance.

When we got to Melody's room, I was relieved to be out of their way, then stunned: two king-sized beds with silk sheets and purple duvets, large windows giving a gorgeous view of the London cityscape, fluffy green carpet, bright blue wallpaper and a large television.

Then there was bathroom, which is equipped with a large bath tub – that I spend thirty minutes in, cleaning my filthy scrawny body – a toilet fit for royalty and a sink that turns on automatically if you put your hands under the tap. The room itself was worth going with Melody, even if she might try to kill me.

Speaking of her, she left a while ago to retrieve someone, and to get me some new clothes – something she insisted on. Shaking my head, I continue my pacing of the hotel room. My wet shaggy caramel hair pulled back in a man-bun, using an elastic band I found on the taxi floor. Why is Melody doing this? Am I a charity case to her?

Before leaving, Melody proclaimed we would be safe for the rest of the day. I can't believe in her Sight; she must be crazy or some bounty hunter my bastard of a father has paid to trap me – like Johnny was.

Sighing, I wonder when she will get back. I'm really thirsty. If I don't feed regularly enough, I can't control how much blood I take.

I don't believe Mum ever liked that I needed to drink blood. Though as a trained nurse she found ways to feed my craving.

Maybe it just reminded her we weren't human. She seldom talked of the supernatural, it was taboo. Of course, there were regular reminders we weren't normal like my dietary need, our supernatural powers and my eyes.

Oh, my eyes, they have always been a reminder of my status. While werewolves have two sets of eyes, their human ones and their secondary werewolf ones that come out when they are emotional, I have just one – like vampires with their blood red irises or magic users, with their peculiar eye colours.

Because vampires and magic users are unable to hide their eyes all the time, the reason humanity doesn't know about us is that their brains simply cannot process the supernatural. Except a certain few.

However, my eyes don't require someone with the ability to see the supernatural. That isn't their only special quality. My eyes always change those who look upon them directly. Some change positively, others negatively, as when people look into my eyes, they have a vision of their death. That's why my whole life, I've needed some form of eye coverings. My current eye-protection, for the last handful of years, has been silver-mirrored, aviator sunglasses.

Stopping my pacing, I sigh sadly. I know I shouldn't exist. A fertility potion was used to bring me into being. Vampires aren't born, they are made, sired from a vampire's blood, and all vampires can be traced back to the First, who was created by an unknown practitioner of magic. So, in reality, I shouldn't exist. The dead can't carry life or sire life, just death. My beating heart proves I am alive.

I remember when Mum told me the story of how they met, how they fell in love, how he flew into a rage after finding out she was pregnant, that he demanded she abort me. I believe she often regretted not doing it. If she had, she would still have been part of her pack, happily soul bonded, and working at the pack clinic.

Some nights, the memories of Mum plague me. I assume she died, I regret not staying and fighting, but it would have been foolish to try. I did not really test what I could do, never pushed my speed or strength to the limit, hell, I didn't even know how to throw a good punch. Mum hated violence, and she always taught me that I had to show restraint, as I could accidentally kill someone by hugging them too hard. It's something I will always have to worry about.

The room's door opens and Melody meanders in, a few brown paper bags in hand and a male hotel employee behind her. He looks a handful of years older than myself, rather cute with his button nose and short blonde hair. He has a badge with his name written on it: Franklin. I don't waste any time. The moment the door shuts, I pin Franklin against the wall and clamp my teeth down onto his soft supple throat.

His rich blood floods my mouth. My body thrums. I could drain him easily, I won't. Even when I was forced to drink from my first person two years ago, I didn't kill her. Franklin is moaning, writhing and clutching at my filthy black hoodie. Gyrating his lower body against me. When a vampire or a half-vampire like myself feeds, venom is injected into their bloodstream, stimulating their nervous system with pleasure. Groaning, I unlatch. The puncture wounds shut immediately with no scarring – my saliva has healing properties.

Forcing his eyes open, I let my sunglasses slip down my nose. His face whitens, a vision of his death playing inside his mind. Ignoring my guilt, I speak in a calm hypnotic voice. "You won't remember anything that just happened. Now go."

Returning my sunglasses to the correct position, I turn to Melody. The sound of the door shutting behind Franklin makes me sad. I yearn to be loved, to be kissed, to be—

Nope, not going any further, don't want to crave something in a different way. Melody has unloaded the contents of the paper bags onto my bed – a plethora of tees, a black hoodie, a handful of comfortable-looking jog bottoms, a few packs of underwear, a pair of combat boots and what looks to be a few hundred dollars.

"You get changed," Melody commands. "I'll wait in the bathroom."

Once she is gone, I speedily discard the filthy, torn and old clothing off my body and dress in a blue tee, the black hoodie, underwear, a comfortable pair of jog bottoms and the combat boots. I ponder how she knew what size I was. Did she – no, this doesn't prove she can see the future; it just means she has a good eye when it comes to clothing and sizes.

Shaking my head, I remove the elastic band and let my wet hair loose. Then run my hands over the soft texture of my new clothing. It has been months since I wore something new – clothing isn't exactly a priority when one is homeless, food and shelter are.

The bathroom door clicks shut as Melody re-enters the room. "You look good," she remarks, and I nod mutely. "You haven't taken the money. You should pocket it."

"Why?" I frown. "It's not like we're in America."

"We will be."

I furrow my brow, how in hell would we get to America? I don't have a passport. Although, I don't bother asking how we will get there. The look on Melody's face is so certain. Wait, we? When did I decide I was going with her? I just wanted a warm place for the night and some blood. I can't give her my trust, like I did Johnny.

The rest of the day passes swiftly. We order room service in the evening, a meal fit for a king. Shortly after that, Melody goes to bed. I don't, I can't. I'm too restless. My mouth is minty-fresh, I've brushed my teeth three times today. I normally only get to brush them once every few days.

Currently, I'm staring out the windows at rain shooting down from the heavens and lightning flashing in the distance. If I was outside, I would have had a very unpleasant night. Melody is fast asleep on her bed; she's probably not working for my father. If she did, she wouldn't dare sleep – she would have waited until I was asleep to attack, like Johnny did – instead, she has left herself vulnerable.

Running my fingers through my shaggy hair, I wonder if I should have it cut. No, I could be out on the street tomorrow. Or I could trust the crazy girl. The idea of trusting her makes me nauseous. I won't let myself be in another Johnny situation, ever again.

"Can't sleep?" Melody asks with a yawn. I wheel around to see she is sitting up on her bed. Her eyes flicker over to the perfectly made bed.

"Couldn't predict I wouldn't sleep, oh great seer?" I retort.

"The future isn't a straight line," she sighs. "There are many possibilities, branching into different and similar timelines. Calculating the likelihood of the timelines, I thought there would be an unlikely chance you wouldn't sleep. Although that doesn't matter. You haven't slept and you really should. We have a big day tomorrow."

"And what is tomorrow?"

"We meet someone."

"Who?" I demand.

Melody sighs tiredly and gets out of bed. The plain red knee-length nightgown she wears has ridden up to her thighs. Biting my bottom lip, I repress thoughts that would make a sailor blush, and my former girlfriend scream in disgust.

Shaking my head, I sit down beside her.

"You don't trust me; I know that, and I know you have good reason. However, you need to trust me. And to answer your question, we are going to meet a witch, so we can acquire her services to open a portal."

"How much will that cost?"

Melody hesitates. "Twenty grand. I have it already in my bag."

My lungs compress. My eyes dart to her bag, which is sat beside mine by the bathroom door; twenty grand is next to my bag. This really is charity.

I could accept her putting me up in a hotel for the night, giving me new clothes, even a few hundred dollars, but for her to spend twenty grand on me!

"Why? Why are you helping me? Why spend twenty grand on me?"

"I need to atone."

"What do you need to atone for?"

She doesn't answer. Minutes pass. I mean, what could she have done?

Finally, she speaks. "My past is something I like to forget. I was kidnapped as a child, taken from England to America. My memories were erased, and my Sight exploited." She pauses, a fleeting bitter expression crosses her face. "A lot of people died because of it. Shadow pack, the pack I was enslaved to, used me to make their pack the strongest in America. A year ago, after a decade of imprisonment, I escaped." Melody's lips quirk into a smile. "I used an attack, organised by a handful of packs, to give me a chance of freedom. If I hadn't managed to escape, I would've been severely punished for not telling my kidnapper about the attack. That was my job, to inform him of future events. His name was Alpha Drake." Melody's face twists into one of disgust at the name of her kidnapper. "I took sanctuary in a nearby pack, and since I couldn't remember my past. They sent my DNA off to the Werewolf Council to see if it matched anyone reported missing."

"Was there a match?" I enquire.

"There was," she says, smiling sorrowfully. "Their kindness helped me reunite with my family and ancestral pack, Reed pack, who had recently relocated to America for a bigger territory. There in Reed pack, I found my soulmate, he had been my best friend before I was taken. His name is Theon Reed." An expression of guilt moulds her features. "However, my happiness wasn't meant to last. Alpha Drake wouldn't let me go, and he still had enough pack members behind him to be a threat. Although, before he would come for me, he wanted me to suffer." Melody takes a few deep breaths. "He made a girl, who unknowingly helped me escape, end her life in front of me. Exterminated the pack that gave me sanctuary, and he would have wiped out Reed pack, if I hadn't done something."

"What did you do?" I ask breathlessly, shocked and numb, transfixed as tears glisten in her eyes. No way is she lying. "How were you able to stop him?"

"I decided to fight back and was able to trigger a vision of the location where Alpha Drake and his pack were. Back then, my Sight was limited to seeing the future, present and past in dreams and visions. So, once I got my chance, I went alone and killed every single person who was part of Alpha Drake's pack, as well as him. There were no children – I'm not a child killer. Nevertheless, children have died because I told Alpha Drake things of the future. Afterwards, I couldn't return, I was a monster, still am." Tears stream down her emotionless face. "I rejected my soulmate; you don't need to be near them to do that. Theon and me, we weren't that close, barely mates for a day, and with our soul bond broken, everyone believes I died."

"You couldn't face them for what you did?"

"No," she agrees, "I couldn't. So, I decided to leave, to travel, to further explore the Sight. I don't dream or have visions anymore, I simply experience it all at once: past, present and future. I once thought being omniscient was impossible. How wrong I was. After a while, I started to help people, to atone for what I have done. I don't feel guilty about it, I don't feel much anymore. I get distracted by all the Sight shows me, and the money, it's nothing, I have millions," she smirks, her tears no longer flowing, "I went to Vegas and within days, I turned fifty dollars into three million. Imagine how much I made in two weeks. Now, do you believe and trust me? I've told you basically my whole life. You know things that no one else does."

I nod. "I believe you, if not, you are one convincing liar, and I mean, if you are, who would have invented such a complicated backstory?"

She laughs emotionlessly. "Thank you for believing in my past, nevertheless you aren't a hundred percent sure about my Sight. Then I will tell you things, using my Sight. For starters, you like girls and guys. You aren't ashamed of liking guys; you just haven't liked a boy enough to date. You have dated. You secretly dated a girl called Sabrina. Red hair, blue eyes. You lost your virginity to her. And finally, when you were six, you found your mum crying in her room, holding a photo of Thomas Blake, your father. It was the first time you had seen a photo of him."

I'm stunned, frozen, I mean she's telling the truth. I'm bisexual. I secretly dated Sabrina. When I was six, I did see Mum crying in her room over a photo of my father. And it was the first time I had seen a photo of him. I believe her. She's a seer, a soothsayer, someone who possesses the Sight, no one could have told her these things.

"I'll go to bed."

"Good," Melody mumbles, and she lies back into her bed.

Heading over to mine, I climb in, not bothering to kick off my new combat boots or remove my sunglasses. I'm used to sleeping with my clothing, sunglasses and footwear on. Maybe Melody will really help me, keep me safe, keep me away from my father and his clan of purists. I'll go with her tomorrow; I just hope I won't regret trusting her.

CHAPTER III

We eat breakfast at the hotel before leaving. Franklin was helping serve the food, and I couldn't help imagining how his body pressed against mine as I fed from him yesterday. How it might have been nice to kiss those lips. I shook that thought away. He didn't recognise me. My compulsion skills are self-taught – didn't know I could do it until I made the first person, I fed from forget it ever happened.

"You ready?" Melody asks, and I nod. She is wearing the tank top from yesterday, but has jeans on instead of leggings, and has ditched her leather jacket.

Once exiting the hotel, we walk south, as the witch lives a few streets away. Melody occasionally points to different people as we go, and reveals things about them, as if she believes she needs to continue to prove her abilities to me.

"He has five children, three of whom his wife doesn't know about."

"She will get hit by a car in thirteen days. There is no escaping it. Her death is a fixed point."

"That boy there, he'll be a famous singer one day."

"See that poor woman, her husband cheats on her."

"That goth guy across the street, he found a dead body when he was a kid. Scarred him—"

Abruptly, Melody stops talking and pauses in front of an old cottage. It doesn't look like it belongs to this street, as all the other homes are townhouses. Plus, the old cottage has a front garden. Its plants are like nothing I have ever seen, some iridescent and others opaque. A stone fence bars the property, its gate open, where a cobblestone path leads to the lime-green front door. People stroll past us, not one of them giving the cottage a glance. They can't see it.

"This is the place," I state.

Melody nods, her eyes distant. I bet she is staring into the future. How fast I've gone from non-believer to accepting her Sight. Still, I may know her motives are atonement, although it doesn't mean I can fully trust her.

Never trust anyone.

I suppress the urge to shiver, Mum always told me that. When I trusted Johnny, I went against that advice. I almost didn't live to regret it.

Some seconds pass, and the door to the cottage opens. Melody's face tints red. "She knows we are here. She wants us to come in."

A knot of unease forms in my stomach, magic users aren't the most trustworthy. Sure, I owe sixteen years of blissful mundane life to a magic user, but they are slippery, dangerous creatures, whom given the chance would sell you out in a second. "Are you sure this is a good idea?"

"We have no choice. There is no other way to get to America, and if you remain in England, even with my help, there is a high chance of getting caught and killed by your father within a week," she pauses, then continues. "This witch isn't trustworthy. In fact, it is highly possible she will contact your father afterwards, and reveal that she opened a portal for us."

"Then what's the point of going to America to escape his reach, when it is highly possible, he'll be told I'm no longer in England?"

"In America, we can get allies."

"Your family and pack," I say, realising her plan. "The ones who think you are dead."

"Yes. I planned not to return, to let them continue thinking I am dead. However, I need their help to save you."

"Why? I know you want atonement; nonetheless, why would you reveal you are alive when you are happy to be dead to them? I mean, I'm not worth it, and it's my life that's on the line."

"Because I see your future. At the moment it is lined with death and danger. However, I see beyond it, I see your soulmate. I see the lives you will save and touch. I see how happy you could become."

"You see all that? I'm no hero, I'm—"

"You aren't an abomination!" she shouts. "You are special and deserve to live."

I blush. "Even if we get rid of my father and his clan, there are hundreds more narrow-minded blood purists. Hell, your family and ex-mate might be purists."

"No, they aren't. From what I've glimpsed of the future, they mainly become distressed and enraged over the fact that I'm alive and lied to them. They will help, help protect you."

"Are you going to leave me there?"

She considers the questions. "Possibly. I'm not sure how my emotions will react to being around them. I let them believe me dead, for I am a monster – someone who took over two hundred lives with their bare hands and felt no remorse."

I shiver. Her blunt statement of killing over two hundred people is chilling. Especially as she claims she did it with her bare hands and feels no remorse about it. "Why do we need them? I mean, you could kill them all?"

"There is little chance we could kill your father and his clan; they are always prepared for an attack. Additionally, your father has been turning humans recently. They now number sixty to seventy vampires, who will follow his every command, and twenty of them are daywalkers. Plus, there is the liability that is you. I couldn't guarantee your safety."

"I didn't realise he had so many followers," I mumble, trying to ignore the sting of being called a liability.

"Yes, so the witch and going to Reed pack is our best option."

"So, be it."

We walk side by side, heading down the cobblestone path, past the strange unknown plants and through the doorway. The door slams behind us as an invisible force pushes us into a living room, where an old grey-haired, pointed nosed, feline-eyed woman sits in a rocking chair. I can't help thinking she looks like a cliché.

The invisible force pushes me down onto a dusty leather sofa, while Melody is propelled onto a waterlogged wooden chair, next to the witch. Wordlessly, Melody pulls her bag off her back and unzips it, retrieving stacks of fifty-pound notes.

The witch takes each fifty-pound stack, and once she has roughly thirteen, she hums in approval and claps her hands. "One portal coming up." Her voice is rough like sandpaper. "Though first, would you like tea?"

Melody doesn't refuse, and as someone who has been homeless for two years, I don't either. You never know when you will get your next food or drink. The witch doesn't stand to get them, a minute goes by when three cups of tea just float into the room. One going to Melody, one to the witch and one to me. I sip the piping hot beverage; it burns my tongue.

"My name is Gretchen, and where will my portal be taking you?" she asks as she loudly takes a swig of her tea, her rocking chair moving to-and-fro. "Italy is lovely this time of year."

"We're going to France," Melody lies, smiling gently in Gretchen's direction. I can tell Melody is about to show me, she's a world-class liar. "Neither of us has passports, and we thought it might be fun to see Paris."

"Two lovebirds then?"

"Nah, he's my brother, and he's into men."

"My grandson is gay." Gretchen smiles fondly. "He married a vampire, his soulmate. I love them both dearly. I am glad neither of them can get pregnant, though. I would hate to have a half-breed in my bloodline."

Great, if she finds out I'm a half-breed, she's definitely going to tell my father. Taking another sip of tea, I wonder if I asked Melody about my soulmate, would she tell me? She said she had seen them. No, I don't think I will, it would be cheating.

Melody directs the conversation back to Paris, talking with fake excitement of all the places she wants to see. I don't seem to need to speak, Gretchen is solely fixed on her. A few more minutes pass, and I place my now empty tea cup on the coffee table. Melody somehow is still talking about Paris; I half expect that to be the real place we are going.

"Can you imagine it?" Melody says. "Me and my brother finding some hot French men to have a romantic holiday fling."

"It is how I met my soulmate, on holiday in Paris. He was a great warlock, passed some years ago," she reveals sadly. "Well, I think that's enough talk. Let me just move the coffee table and I'll open the portal. I assume you know how they work?"

"No, our parents recommended we try it, since we don't have passports, and the last time we went on an aeroplane, we had a terrible time, the plane almost crashed! And we both get horrible sea sickness when it comes to boats. So, portal travel felt like the right way to go."

"Portals are a good way to travel. It is rather simple. I open a portal, you two hold hands, and one of you thinks of a place you wish to go, then you step through."

Melody flashes Gretchen a grateful smile, as if she is some thankful clueless girl. Gretchen accepts this and moves the coffee table from the middle of the room. Once that is accomplished, she begins to chant in a peculiar lyrical language. Raising her hands above her head, her floral dress flutters as if a great wind is around her. Then in a flash of white light, a shimmering bluish doorway forms in front of her. Gretchen stops her chanting, drops her arms, and seems as if she will return to her chair, when her slitted feline-like eyes meet mine. She stiffens, the colour in her face vanishing.

"You aren't normal. You're a half-breed, half-vampire and half-werewolf. Your blood sings it painfully loud, how did I not hear it?" Gretchen whimpers, shaking as she retreats to the doorway. "Your eyes, though, don't belong to a hybrid like you. Magic is woven in those eyes, forging a connection to the Source."

I frown. "What do you mean magic is woven in my eyes? And what is the Source I supposedly have a connection to?"

"Your ignorance disgusts me," she sneers, her terror replaced with anger. "Although I will answer your questions. Now tell me, how were you conceived and were any spells cast on you in the womb?"

"My Mum used a fertility potion," I state stiffly, "and a ritual was performed on Mum while I was in the womb to keep us hidden."

"As I expected," she says, spitting on the floor. I bet she wanted her spit to land on my face. "I theorise that you absorbed magic into your eyes, while you were maturing in the womb. By absorbing the magic into your eyes, it has formed a weak connection to the Source, giving you the ability to show people's deaths. And for your information, the Source is where magic originates. I mean, did you really think your eyes were normal? Just part of your hybrid physiology? No, it is mutation, a dangerous one that has shown me how I could die. For I saw it in your eyes, when I used my magic to look through your sunglasses."

Tears begin to appear in her eyes, and I want to be sick. I did not question why my eyes were so strange. I knew that a warlock did the ritual on Mum and me while I was in the womb. I thought nothing of it. Now I know different – my eyes are a side-effect. I'm not a normal hybrid. Melody had said earlier. *You are special.* She knew, she knew that my eyes were an accidental mutation.

"We should be going," Melody states, standing. She seems utterly calm, the excited holiday-goer gone, and back is the indifferent all-knowing seer. Taking her lead, I stand too, Gretchen watches me, stepping back further, scared of me, scared of my eyes. It reminds me of how Mum acted when she accidentally looked into my eyes. Pale, scared and horrified. Repressing the memories, Melody laces her fingers with mine. I want to demand why she didn't tell me about my eyes, although I could guess the answers. *You didn't ask* or *best to hear it from her.*

"Tell Thomas Blake, when he comes," Melody says swiftly, "that his son is under my protection, and we will be waiting for him in Paris."

"You aren't going to Paris," Gretchen hisses. "If I hadn't seen his eyes or listened to his blood song, I wouldn't have doubted your story," shaking her head, she crosses her arms. "He's a disgusting abomination that should not exist! The single reason he does exist is because of a potion!"

"Who are you to judge what should exist?" Melody shouts back, before speaking in a calm voice. "All I can do is plead you don't talk or contact his father. Though, I know that is unlikely." Gretchen stares at Melody in puzzlement, I can't blame her. "Now, goodbye, we will be going."

Melody steps through the portal, dragging me through with her. It is a strange sensation; my ears pop and I feel like I am spinning really fast. For a moment, we stand in darkness, then abruptly the surroundings change, and we are standing outside a twenty-four-seven, Wild West themed American diner called: Wild Pete's Adventurous Diner.

CHAPTER IV

Reed pack is close, in fact if we were to head into the forest surrounding this town, we would be in their territory. Melody, however, told me it wasn't the right time, and we should get a hotel and rest up a bit, since they would all be asleep. I could tell that was the truth. Still, I could also tell she just wanted to put it off for a bit too.

So, here we are in a small, cheap hotel room with one bed and a dingy, dirty bathroom. Melody fell asleep instantly. I don't, I lie awake. Sleep has not been something I need much of, nor do I like to sleep in the presence of others, not since Johnny.

The sun is beginning to rise. America is hours behind England, and I never thought I would go abroad. Strange to think I am so very far away from the place I grew up.

The town Melody has brought us to is called Lockborough, and is located in the state of Maine. There was a pamphlet in the hotel lobby that detailed Lockborough's founding in 1896 by James Lock.

Soundlessly, I rise from bed and locate my bag. Unzipping it, I dig through the contents to find a small photograph – the only photograph I have of Mum and me. It is old, ripped in the corners and a lot of the colour has faded. I'm eleven in the photo, hugging

Mum with the silver-mirrored aviator sunglasses on my nose, that were slightly too large for my pre-pubescent face. I'm still wearing the sunglasses to this day, though I've grown into them now. Mum had just given them to me a few minutes before the photo was taken.

Studying her, the already familiar image, I take in her smile, her blonde hair pulled back into a lazy bun and her vibrant green eyes full of love directed at me. Our neighbour took the photo, but I don't remember his name. I would just call him dude if we spoke.

Shaking my head, I am eternally grateful Mum always insisted on having go-bags stashed about Oxstead. If she hadn't, I would have been a runaway with just the clothing on my back. The bag I had grabbed was buried at the Oxstead's town welcome sign; the photo was a surprise. A lovely surprise. The last gift she ever gave me.

Flipping the photo to the back, I read the familiar words. *Clay, I love you, I will always love you. Survive for me, my sweet boy.* Grief and remorse wash over me. I will always hear her yelling, *Run, my sweet boy, run,* always.

"Coward," I whisper. "Fool."

Shutting my eyes, I imagine what Father and his clan did to her. I pray they gave her a quick death. Forcing myself, I stumble over to the bed and shake Melody, waking her.

Her dark brown eyes open, piercing through my very soul. She knows what I want to ask already. Nevertheless, I put my thoughts into words. "Did they make her suffer? Was she granted a quick death?"

"No – it wasn't quick."

"Then she really must have regretted not aborting me. How could she not regret the thing that cost her own life?"

"A mother's love is a powerful thing, Clay," Melody reassures me. "And she loved you dearly."

Blinking away tears, I look away. "Can you tell me if I stayed and fought – would she have lived?"

"No," Melody says, no room for disagreement. "You would have simply died, and you are destined for more than that."

"Because of my freaky mutant eyes connected to the Source?"

"In part, yes," Melody sits up, "they make you special. Those who look into your eyes see their death. It changes people, and you have more talents, talents best learnt by yourself."

"Would it be a spoiler?" I deadpan.

"I suppose it would. I could tell you so much. Information that would boggle and fracture your mind."

A question pops into my head, and without thinking I ask, "Would you give it up? Give up your Sight, give up being omniscient."

A bitter sad expression befalls her face. "It is my duty to use my Sight to help people. It would be selfish if I wished I could not. When I was Alpha Drake's prisoner, he made me feel that I needed to be omniscient, but I couldn't. And because I wasn't omniscient, I could not save Holly pack, a pack that gave me shelter. And their reward was death. I guess that's why after killing Alpha Drake and his pack, I decided to master my Sight. To truly become omniscient. I thought it impossible to accomplish yet I succeeded and I see everything. Would I give up my Sight, no, no I wouldn't, it is a burden I must carry – one my Goddess thrust upon me."

"Melody," I say sadly, "you are selfless and strong."

I don't think she believes me, since the bitter sorrowful smile remains. "I am just a girl with great power that needs to atone for her past."

My heart aches painfully. "Will you ever be able to really atone?"

"I don't think I can," Melody frowns, "so many people died because of me – children died. I see them, all those I got killed. The ones who died, because I told Alpha Drake the future. The ones Alpha Drake killed, because I escaped, and the ones I killed, because they were part of Alpha Drake's pack. Nevertheless, I don't feel remorse for killing them or guilt for being used or escaping."

"I think that's a lie," I argue. "I think you are lying to yourself Melody. If that was true, you wouldn't force yourself to atone. You wouldn't feel the need to atone."

Melody laughs emotionlessly. "Maybe you are right. Doesn't change anything. I must atone."

The urge to slap her arises. She gave up her family, a mate and a pack, because she felt like a monster. If she feels no guilt or remorse, why force herself to atone by helping people – helping me? No words depart from my lips. There is nothing I can say to convince her she isn't a monster. I just pray one day someone can convince her.

I manage a quick nap, then we eat brunch in *Wild Pete's Adventurous Diner*. The staff are all dressed as cowboys or cowgirls. Once we finish, we head into Reed territory.

It is midday, and the sun is high in the sky. Melody is eerily quiet as we move through the woods, not a leaf or stick breaking under foot. Me, on the other hand, I'm like a bull in a china shop.

I can tell Melody is nervous, her heart is beating crazily.

Part of me wonders if someone will attack me. My scent leans towards my vampiric side, and everyone knows vampires and werewolves get along like religion and science – not well at all.

Mum said she and Father were the exception to the rule, and both her pack and his clan were supportive of their union – until I came along. She did not tell me what her family or pack's reaction to her pregnancy was. Though, I doubt it was good, if it meant she needed a ritual to keep us hidden. Over the last two years, I half expected Mum's old pack to start hunting me too.

"We're close to her," Melody whispers, "she will lead us to the pack house."

"Couldn't you just take us there?"

"Yeah, dead girl and a hybrid walk up to the pack house where children are playing on the porch, what could go wrong?"

I clamp my mouth shut and blush. She's right. It was stupid of me to think we could march straight to the pack house. Walking a while longer, we emerge into a small meadow where a short, thin twenty-something woman is crouched on the ground, dressed in jog bottoms and a sweatshirt.

It takes a few moments until she notices us. Upon doing so, she springs to her feet, spins around, orange eyes glowing, her fingernails extending into claws as she half-shifts. Even in this state, she's pretty with symmetrical features, light brown skin and short brown hair.

Almost instantly, when she registers Melody, her Delta eyes disappear, replaced with her human grey ones. Her claws vanish too, as an angry expression forms on her face.

"No body was found," she says, her accent strongly British. "You let everyone believe you were dead. Your brother, your mum, even Theon. You knew his greatest fear was losing you and becoming broken. What type of person does that? Bring someone's greatest fear to life?"

"A bad one," Melody replies hollowly.

"Yes, a bad person, you let us all think you were dead. I can't stand to look at you," her gaze flits to me for an instant, eyes flashing orange, before returning to Melody. "Why are you back?"

"My friend, Clay, needs help."

"Let him get help from his own kind." I flinch, I have no kind, are there any other living hybrids at the moment? "If that's all, then flee, let everyone else continue to believe you are dead."

Melody's fingers curl into fists, her bottom lip quivering briefly. Cathy's eyes move back onto her. "I came to you, Cathy, as you were the most likely not to over react emotionally. It seems I made a mistake."

"Fuck yes, you were wrong. We didn't spend much time together, but I liked you. Thought we might become friends. I also hoped you would make my cousin happy. Instead, he mourned you!"

"It was better that way," Melody dismisses. "I was no longer worthy of him, of any of you. I killed them all. I killed the guards on patrol first, then I snuck into the tents and killed them while they slept. I saved him for last, Alpha Drake, and he said it best. I am his daughter, he raised me, and I became a monster – just like him. So, I decided I couldn't go back, I can't go back. Nevertheless, I must for Clay, or his own father will kill him. Just because he's half-vampire and half-werewolf."

Cathy's eyes flick back to me, and softness-forms in them. "He can stay. I'm sure my uncle, Alpha Andrew, will help."

"Good."

Silence settles over the small meadow; Melody could leave me. Cathy herself said I could stay, that her uncle will help. Yet, I don't want to see her go; I don't want to lose the first person I've been able to trust in the last two years. Someone worthy of my trust, unlike Johnny, who wasn't.

I know I don't need to tell her, for she is looking at me, a smile on her lips, she already knows what I want to tell her. Tears itch at my eyes, Melody Morning is my friend and my saviour. My mouth opens to vocalise these things when a strange expression settles on her face.

"What's wrong?"

"I can't see anything," she says, her voice full of fear. "I can't see the future. Something is—" A gunshot rings out, birds fly out of trees, and the scent of blood blooms in the small meadow, "—wrong with my Sight."

Another shot goes off. Cathy hit the ground upon the first shot and is army crawling towards the tree-line.

I'm frozen, staring at Melody in horror. She was shot in the gut first, then the shoulder, both wounds drenching her yellow tank top. A third shot echoes loudly, this time squarely hitting Melody above her cleavage. Snapping out of it, I dive forwards, tackling Melody to the ground. Then begin dragging her limp bleeding body behind a tree.

Melody isn't conscious, her head lolls forwards, her three gun-shot wounds have ruined her tank top. Why does that seem important? I must be in shock.

The seer, who claimed to be omniscient, has been blindsided and shot thrice. Her heart is slowing. She will die.

My throat burns, my self-control wavering at all the blood. I want to feed off my dying friend. What type of person am I? *An abomination.* A voice inside my head answers. *You can't save her. You couldn't save your mother.*

Whimpering, I listen, so many heart beats. Many are coming this way. Though one is too calm, too relaxed, too close. The shooter.

I have not directly killed anyone. For Melody, I might give it a go.

"Don't."

I flinch, Melody is awake, her right hand grasps my left wrist weakly.

"Stay with me please. I don't want to die alone. Please, Clay."

I can't refuse. My fury vanishes, replaced with sorrow. "You'll live. You'll heal."

"I'm not healing."

She is right, her bleeding hasn't slowed down. "Have faith."

"Maybe this is what I deserve," blood begins to dribble down her chin. "Maybe, my atonement is death."

CHAPTER V

The water cascades onto me, washing her blood down the drain. The gunshots ring in my head, over and over. *Coward*. If I had moved faster, reacted better, she would have only been shot once, not thrice. Futilely, I blink away tears. Not that anyone would see. My mind drifts, I do not want it to, but it does.

They took Melody. One of them snarled at me, a mixture of shock, rage, relief, confusion and love shining in his luminous red eyes. Her ex-mate. None of them touched or spoke to me.

After an hour of sitting in the dirt alone, numb to the world, Cathy came back. She first informed me she had explained what happened. Next, she told me that Melody was in a critical condition. Her life is up to the Goddess and their pack doctors' hands.

Then, she helped me up and we began walking. It took a few minutes to reach the pack house. It is built in a clearing, the structure made of red brick, five stories with a porch, a green tiled roof, and behind the structure is a training ground, a large tarmac square where several pack members were engaged in combat. There was also a small building next to the pack house, reeking of blood and disinfectant – a clinic.

The porch had childish chalk drawings, one of them was of a stick figure that made me think of Melody. And suddenly I was back there again. *"Maybe this is what I deserve,"* blood begins to dribble down her chin. *"Maybe, my atonement is death."*

Coming back to myself, I switch off the shower, sit down, hug my knees to my chest and sob. Cathy insisted I use her shower to get clean. I wish I hadn't. Melody's dried blood could have been a reminder of her. How could I care so much about Melody in the time I've known her? *She saved you.* The voice is back again. *And look what it got her. An abomination like you would be better off dead.*

I want to howl in rage, I want to drink blood until my pain fades. I want – someone to hold me. My crying slows and I force myself out of the shower cubicle. I stumble in front of the sink, my eyes unwilling to see the reflection. Yet I know what I would see. I know my appearance inside and out. I have shaggy caramel hair, pointed inhuman canines, making me look like a classic vampire with fangs; unnaturally white skin, thanks to my vampiric heritage and freaky eyes – the slitted pupils are white, the irises the colour of darkness, and my sclera, which is normally white in humans, is blood red for me.

Abomination eyes. I should claw them out.

You are special.

I gasp, her voice, the memory of it makes me want to cry again. Melody doesn't think I'm an abomination, and she saw all, well almost all. Bile rises to my throat. Her shooter got away. I should have chased her or him and killed them.

A knock comes from the door. "It's me, Cathy. Umm Dylan, Melody's brother, dropped by while you were showering. He said she is in recovery and stable."

"That's good news," I croak, my voice strained.

"I'm just going to get coffee, then we can go see her. You can meet Melody's Mum."

I grunt, not trusting my voice. Moving slowly, I dress in my blue tee – a few flecks of blood on the neckline – a new pair of jog bottoms, the combat boots and my silver-mirrored, aviator sunglasses. The black hoodie and former jog bottoms were both ruined by mud, dirt and blood.

Exiting the bathroom, taking my bag with me, I sit on Cathy's bed, and the memory of Melody replays in my head again. *"Maybe this is what I deserve,"* blood begins to dribble down her chin. *"Maybe, my atonement is death."*

Wiping traitorous tears, I wonder why am I so weak? I'm a hybrid with freaky mutated eyes – yet I'm useless. I ran when Mum needed me, and I reacted too slowly when Melody needed it.

"You couldn't have done anything to stop it," Cathy says. I jump, not realising she had returned with her coffee. "And you pulled Melody to safety. You saved her."

"Too late," I reply. "I saved her too late. I should have saved her after the first shot – not the third."

Cathy sighs. "If it's your fault, then it's mine too. I was in the meadow."

"You weren't standing next to her."

"I was there."

"It isn't the same thing."

"Fine," Cathy huffs, "if you want the blame, keep it. Now come on, your friend is waiting in the clinic."

I nod and we leave her room. I had noticed earlier that all the doors in the hall, and the halls we passed once we went upstairs, had plaques with names on them. I didn't notice last time, but at the end of this hall is one that reads *Melody Morning/Sam Winters.* Her room and maybe her real name? Sam Winters, it suits her.

Shaking that realisation away, I follow Cathy through the halls, down the stairs, out of the pack house and into the clinic. Inside the clinic is a long hall with lots of doors. Cathy stops in front of room seventeen, pushing it open, I see Melody in a hospital gown, a blanket pulled up to her chest, her skin ghostly white.

A woman stands over her, dragging a wet cloth over her forehead. She has Melody's dark brown eyes and has grey hair in a loose braid. She must be Melody's Mum. The man, who must be Melody's brother, sits on the other side of the hospital bed in an uncomfortable-looking plastic chair. He has coal black hair styled in a quiff, an upturned nose, tanned skin and emerald green eyes.

Standing here, in the doorway to Melody's hospital room, I wonder if I deserve to be here. I'm not family, and we've only known each, maybe twenty-four hours. I didn't even know her real name might be Sam Winters.

As I take a step back, Melody's Mum looks up at me, her dark brown eyes directed into my soul. "You must be Clay, the one my daughter was trying to protect. I'm Ashley Winters, her mum, and this is her brother. I know if anything by your face, you are feeling guilty. Don't. You saved her."

Mutely, I nod my head. So, Melody's birth name is Sam Winters, not Melody Morning. I'm not entirely sure if I believe her mother, that I shouldn't feel guilty. I acted too slowly. Stepping into the room, Cathy shuts the door behind her, then pulls a plastic chair towards me, so I can sit down.

"I'm Dylan," the brother tells me as I flop into the chair. "Thank you so much for saving her."

"It was nothing."

"No, it was everything."

"It really is," Ashley sighs tiredly. "Now, let's pray to the Goddess." Cathy first puts her coffee on the floor, then we all join hands, our heads bowing. "Goddess, hear our prayers, heed our plea, spare my beloved daughter. Please, Goddess, give her a chance to live. She deserves more than the eighteen years she's been given. Amen."

"Amen," we mutter in unison. Looking up, I stare at Melody, a maelstrom of guilt swirling inside me. I hope she makes it – that she survives. If she doesn't, I'll never forgive myself. Goddess, please heed our prayer, please...

CHAPTER VI

A day passes rapidly, and another begins. Today is the day I should have died if Melody – or Sam – had not intervened. I have left her side only when I needed to use the toilet or grab a snack, or in one case, to grab a blood bag a pack doctor said I could have.

A lot of different people visited Melody, the most recurring being her ex-mate, Theon Reed, Alpha Andrew's son.

I didn't take in Theon's appearance when I first saw him, mainly because I was in shock. Now, I know his attractive face well. He has black hair that matches the same shade as Melody's, his bronze skin seems to glow, his eyes are sickly blue and he's quite muscular, as his tees always seem to outline every muscle.

Another visitor is Jared Winters, Dylan's mate and husband, an Omega with curly red hair, grass green eyes and milky white skin. Also, a Gamma named William visited frequently, who is soul bonded to the Beta of this pack. His official title is Beta-Male, the counterpart of the Beta like an Alpha has a counterpart, which is normally the Alpha-Female.

I've conversed with Dylan and Ashley a lot, the two of them are Delta werewolves. Like me, they seldom leave Melody's side. From the talks, I learned Dylan and Jared have a preteen adopted daughter, Katie.

Melody has woken up a few times, held conversations, although each time she's terrified and mumbles she can't see. We all know what she means – somehow her Sight is gone. A few hours ago, the pack doctors decided Melody was good enough to be moved to her bedroom. The moment we entered the room, the scent of her ex-mate was overpowering – it smelt as if he was still in the room.

Dylan had left at that point, deciding to spend some time with Jared and Katie, leaving me with Ashley. Each time Melody wakes up, she remarks that Ashley hasn't cried. I know why she says that, as Ashley told me that when Melody returned to her, her mate had died six months before, and she was constantly in a state of emotions that caused her to cry frequently.

Between the believed-to-be-dead daughter returned to her and the dead soulmate, it is understandable. When Ashley believed her daughter dead again, she vowed not to shed a tear ever again, a vow she has kept to this day.

I snap out of my thoughts as Alpha Andrew steps into the room. He isn't muscular, but lean like a swimmer and dark-skinned; his hair has fallen out, leaving him bald, and his eyes are a light shade of brown.

Alpha Andrew and myself have talked a bit, mainly the reason I need his protection, how I survived on the streets and what my life was like before with my mum. Graciously, he has given me pack protection, so I am safe here.

"A neighbouring pack will visit in an hour," Alpha Andrew states calmly. "It might be best if you remain here. I'd rather not find out how my fellow Alpha feels about hybrids."

"Good idea," I agree.

Alpha Andrew's gaze flicks to Ashley and her heart rate spikes. "Is Melody doing well?"

"She is," Ashley replies.

"That's great. Hopefully she will recover fully. My son might stop by in a bit. Please tell me, he hasn't got in the way of anything."

"No, he hasn't," she says. "Though, it is surprising he can break away from her side."

"It is surprising," he agrees. "Best go now, many preparations to be made."

Once Alpha Andrew is gone, I throw Ashley a teasing smile. She blushes bright crimson. It seems Alpha Andrew and Ashley Winters may be a thing. Who would have thought.

Forty minutes later, Theon visits Melody. He even manages a short conversation with her. Nothing big. She's scared and promises she will be staying. I think she's feeling all the emotions she's been repressing.

Also, she's terrified her Sight will not return and nothing will soothe that worry. For no one knows how she could have lost her Sight. Though, I have a sinking suspicion the shooter might be the cause. Melody couldn't see him or her. What if they somehow stole her abilities?

Shaking my head, I stand, Ashley is in bed with Melody sleeping peacefully. I wonder how long I was lost in thought. I don't remember Theon leaving, so I guess it must have been a while.

Stretching, my heart begins to pound. I don't know why and frown as I hear heavy footsteps approaching. Turning to the door, I half expect it to be ripped off the hinges revealing a growling snarling beast on the other side.

Instead, the door swings open to reveal a muscular man – a man more handsome than anyone I had ever seen. He has a square jaw, defined cheekbones, black hair in a buzz-cut, a Roman nose, stormy grey eyes and sun-kissed skin. He wears loose jog bottoms, black trainers and a taut black tee over his broad shoulders. His scent is very enticing, and I fight the urge to throw myself at him and drain him dry.

"Mate," the man snarls, his eyes flashing luminous red.

My heart splutters, this man in front of me is my soulmate, and I haven't changed in the last two days or brushed my hair. I must look a mess. "Hi," I squeak out, a tidal wave of emotion swirling into our brand-new soul bond, "I'm Clay."

"You are mine," he says in his American-accented, deep masculine voice. "I'm Alpha Liam of Willow pack, and you will be coming with me. I'll be back." And with that, he marches away. There was no room to argue, it was a fact that I would go with him.

The moment the door closes behind him, I feel a pair of eyes on me – Melody. She's awake again, staring at me with her so different dark brown eyes, now full of helplessness. "At least I correctly predicted you would meet him here," she mumbles. "And you will go with him."

"But—"

"No," Melody snarls. "No buts. You will go with him. I can no longer help you; I am helpless. And plus, Willow pack is the fifth strongest in America, Reed pack is the fifteenth."

"But I don't want to abandon you. You are my friend."

Melody sighs. "What did I say about the buts?" Pausing, she shakes her head, then she goes on. "You will make other friends and you'll have him. He will die for you, and we both know the one thing you've craved over the last two years is someone who loves you and will hold you. Alpha Liam is that man, your man."

"You are in danger," I try to argue.

"I have a pack, family and ex-mate to look after me. I don't need you too."

The words sting; she doesn't need me. "I want to pay you back for what you have done for me. You saved my life; I would be dead today if you hadn't found me."

"I would be dead if you hadn't pulled me to safety. We've paid each other back, my friend. It is time we go our separate ways. You deal with the danger looming over you, I'll deal with mine."

"This won't be the last time I'll see you, Sam?"

"Don't call me that," she snaps, eyes shining luminous silver. "I'm Melody Morning. I don't deserve the name of that girl. She was good and had no blood on her hands, not the oceans that cover my palms now. I am what Alpha Drake made me, I am Melody Morning, his daughter."

My heart breaks for her. "I'm sorry, Melody."

"It's fine, and I'm sorry for snapping," her eyes return to normal. "And to answer your previous question, I know this isn't the last time we will meet."

"How can you be so sure?"

"A gut feeling."

Melody's eyes close, and I know that our conversation is over. She must rest again. Locating my bag, I sling it over my back. Melody is right, I will go with Alpha Liam, and that she can no longer be of use to me. For Melody is bedridden, powerless and her gunshot wounds will take a while to heal, as they are healing the human way. Plus, she has enough drama here to deal with, she doesn't need mine too. As Father and his clan will come for me. It could be days, weeks, or years, but he will come. Will Alpha Liam really risk his pack to protect me? A hybrid with freaky mutated eyes, connected to the Source.

Ashley mumbles in her sleep, pulling Melody closer to her body. What role would I play in Willow pack? I am Alpha Liam's mate, so that would make me Alpha-Male, the counterpart of the Alpha, but that role is normally the Alpha-Female. Gosh, what if his pack won't accept that Alpha Liam's mate is a dude?

I can't do this! At least three days ago, I knew how to live my life on the streets.

Also, what is life in a pack going to be like? I didn't experience anything here in Reed pack. I did not part from Melody's side. I can't go, I just can't. I hate attention; I was the guy in school whose name teachers and peers struggled to remember. I liked that; it meant I was mundane to them.

"You should breathe," a voice comments. I spin around to see Theon Reed, leaning in the doorway. "Alpha Liam wants you to come outside. He's waiting with his Beta and the pack warriors he brought."

"I thought he was coming to collect me?"

"I convinced him to let me do it. Give my father more time to explain your situation."

"And it is a fun situation."

He laughs quietly. "Don't worry, he won't turn you away, no mate would do that – except maybe me. For Melody and me, we broke our soul bond the moment we were reunited. She was my childhood best friend, no one replaced her when she was taken. A few days later, after we rejected each other, we repaired it," he sighs sadly. "All it takes to heal a broken soul bond is a kiss and on that same day, she broke that bond again, making me and everyone think she died," he wipes away his tears. "Have you said your goodbyes to Melody?"

"I have," I answer awkwardly, "she wants me to go. She thinks I don't need to stay as I've paid her back already."

"You have, you saved her, brought her back to me too. I'm so grateful that she decided to help you, otherwise I would never have known she was alive."

"Do you plan to get back together with her?" I pry. "Reunite your status as her mate, instead of ex-mate? I know it isn't any of my business."

"I'll allow your prying, and yes, I do. I'm angry she faked her death, let me mourn her, let me break inside, but nonetheless, she is the one – my soulmate."

"Some soulmate I am, you deserve more," Melody says weakly. At some point, she must have regained consciousness again. "I'm a monster – a powerless, useless monster. You don't need me. For I saw in the future that you would find love again, a woman who you deserve, who would give you beautiful children."

"I don't care about her," he snaps. "I care about my flawed, beautiful, strong soulmate." He goes to Melody, kneeling down to her.

Melody pushes Ashley away and sits up, an expression of pain filtering across her face. "How am I beautiful? I'm in a hospital gown and sickly white. Not to mention I'm at the weakest I've ever been."

"Melody, you are always strong, and your beauty will not fade. I cried every night at the loss of you, like my father did my mother. I want our happily ever after, you deserve it after everything you've been through."

"I don't deserve happiness," Melody weeps. "I'm a—"

"No," Theon interrupts, like Melody had done to me days ago. "You aren't a monster. A monster would not have been hurt as you have been in the past. Your atonement is over, maybe that is why the Goddess has revoked your Sight. For she has seen that you deserve some peace. Something you have never known."

They kiss, both crying and hugging each other, as if they are the only two people in the world. All the while, Ashley sleeps soundlessly, unaware of the events that have transpired.

CHAPTER VII

I head downstairs and outside on my own, opting to leave Melody and Theon to continue their make-out session alone, well, alone as one can get with Ashley asleep in the bed with Melody.

Alpha Andrew is speaking to Alpha Liam, my soulmate. It feels surreal. A cluster of werewolves are behind them. A skinny, curly blonde male splits out of the cluster of werewolves and runs towards me, his green eyes excited. "Alpha-Male Clay, I'm JJ, Alpha Liam's Beta, it is an honour to meet you," he says in an American accent. I'm going to have to get used to hearing Americans. Jared and William were the single two Americans I interacted with during my stay here – everyone else was British. "Let me take your bag, then I'll introduce you to some of the guys."

Slowly, I hand over my bag, half-expecting him to run off with it. Don't let anyone get hold of your belongings – I learned that the hard way. He doesn't, instead we stroll over to the cluster of werewolves and he begins naming them. Each of them throwing a polite smile my way and congratulating me on what should be a happy union between myself and Alpha Liam.

If any of them addressed me, it was always by Alpha-Male. I tried to hide my discomfort at the title, although I knew I wasn't fooling anyone. A few minutes pass before we depart. No one speaks as we hike through Reed territory.

When we escape the woods, we head towards *Wild Pete's Adventurous Diner.* It is closed and there are three vehicles parked up front, two vans and a Range Rover. The others briskly pile into the two vans and drive off, while Alpha Liam and myself get into the Range Rover alone. Switching on the ignition, he lets the engine idle, it feels strange to be alone together.

"My territory is ten minutes away. It isn't that far, since our territory is in the same forest as Reed pack," Alpha Liam informs me in a cold voice. "The forest spans eleven miles in every direction from Lockborough. Four packs claim territory in the forest: Reed pack, Willow pack, Johnson pack and Miller pack. When Reed pack relocated here three years ago, my pack was the only one to offer an alliance. Now Johnson pack is the sole one holding out. I understand why. This land, this forest, has been ours for centuries, and they just came and claimed a chunk of it. Sure, it was considered unclaimed territory, a majority of the forest is, but that's done to keep us separate, so we aren't fighting for borders," he pauses, gasping for air. "I don't know why I've told you all that, it was probably rather boring for you."

"It was interesting," I reply nervously. "I don't know much about packs or their politics."

"You will learn, you are the Alpha-Male to my Alpha."

"Am I what you hoped for?"

"You mean, did I want a man as my soulmate?"

My face blazes and I nod shyly.

"Yes, I did," he laughs, he seems to relax, the coldness in his voice vanishing. "I'm gay, known it since I was an eleven-year-old crushing on all the hot male celebs. Were you hoping for a man?"

"I'm bisexual, so I just hoped you would like me."

"I do like you. Though I won't lie, and say I didn't imagine a hybrid as my mate."

"You're not a blood purist, are you?" I worry aloud.

"Of course not," he scoffs. "Neither is anyone in my pack. There are just stories about hybrids, painting them as wild cruel killing-obsessed beasts. I never thought I would meet one."

"I'm no beast," I state resentfully, "and I haven't killed anyone."

"I wasn't trying to say that," he says, attempting to backtrack.

"I know. But you said it, did you not?"

"I'm sorry," his hand clasps mine, and I feel through our fledgling soul bond that he feels shame, remorse and embarrassment. "I wasn't trying to say you were a beast, just that there are stories." His other hand cups my face, and my heart begins to run at the speed of light. "Can I see your eyes?"

"You don't want to see them." I frown, bitterness lacing my words, "it will hurt you. Alpha Andrew must have told you about that. As well as about my murderous father and his clan of purists?"

"Of course, he did. Alpha Andrew told me about you and your situation. It changes nothing between us. Still, I wish to see your eyes."

Hesitantly and furtively, I remove my sunglasses. Fearful to see his reaction. My eyes stare into the depths of his stormy grey eyes. He doesn't pale or look away; Alpha Liam just stares back. My eyes seemingly have no effect on him.

"Your eyes are definitely unique. Yet, they hold no power over me. All I see is you, my mate. I guess, I'm immune."

I blink away unshed tears, no one in my life has been able to look me in my eyes and just see me. Both his hands cup my face, his nose brushes against mine, our exhales of breath fanning one another's faces.

"I will protect you – until my dying day," he promises. "You are my family, my blood and my heart."

"What if... I'm not worth all the trouble?"

"You are the keeper of my heart. You are worth it," his lips meet mine, the kiss gentle, innocent and fleeting with promises of more. "You are mine, Clay."

And I know he means it; I feel his emotions through our soul bond. Pressing a brief kiss against his lips, I sit back and fasten the seat belt, Alpha Liam doing the same. Putting my sunglasses back on, I flinch inwardly as he places his hand back on my cheek.

"When we are alone, you don't need to wear them."

"I don't," I agree, giddy at the knowledge.

"If it is alright," Alpha Liam hesitates, "would you be comfortable sleeping in my room?"

My heart summersaults. For some reason, I just know he isn't like Johnny. "I wouldn't mind."

He smiles, and it seems to light up his whole face. That smile could make me do anything. I always wondered what a soulmate was like. Mum could never find the words to describe it, but now I know. It feels as if we have known each other our whole lives, that we have not truly lived until just now. This is the feeling of a soulmate, the feeling he has awakened in me.

Willow pack isn't that far, I would say it takes less than ten minutes. Once we were outside Lockborough, Alpha Liam drove up a dirt road, which he told me was enchanted to keep humans from seeing it.

The road takes us all the way to the pack house, which is located in a large clearing. It is almost identical to Reed's pack house, made of red brick, five stories with a porch and a blue tiled roof instead of green.

Behind the pack house, I glimpse a training ground just like Reed pack has behind them, though different, as I spotted an obstacle course. But the major differences between Reed pack and Willow pack are that there are four structures in the clearing, instead of Reed pack's two. One of the structures is a garage, where we parked the Range Rover between four vans. The other two are a log cabin and a big clinic that reeks more powerfully of blood and disinfectant than Reed Packs'. The garage and the clinic are on the right side of the pack house, and the log cabin is on the left of it.

After locking up the garage, we retreat to the treeline so I can take it all in. People mill about in the clearing, some are kids playing games, others are talking in small groups. Five minutes must pass until Alpha Liam breaks the silence between us. "The garage is used to store our vehicles, as you've seen. The building next to it is the clinic, where we treat the sick or injured, and the log cabin is where I – we will sleep and live," a light blush dusts his cheeks. "The pack house's layout is rather simple. Floors five, four and three are just bedrooms, the first and second floors have kitchens and recreational rooms. Just on the first floor we have a ballroom, a few bathrooms, a library, storage rooms, Beta JJ's office and my future heir's office. I got rid of mine; I do all my work in the log cabin. My grandparents built it and my parents lived there when they were younger."

"Why did they move out?"

"When they started having kids."

"You have siblings?"

He grimaces. "Yes, I had two older brothers. But four years ago, my parents and older brothers, Peter and Freddie, died in a packless attack. I was fourteen. That was the day I became Alpha of Willow pack. Like I was born to be," he sighs sadly, his eyes distant. "Peter wasn't an Alpha, he took after my mom, who was a Delta and Freddie was an Omega, taking after our distant great-grandpa. Odd how genetics work. You never know who you'll take after. One of your parents or a distant relative. Anyway, if I'd died, Willow pack would have ceased to exist. A pack needs an Alpha."

I nod, feeling a bit clueless. "I'm sorry about what happened. I wish you didn't have to lose them."

"Why? You didn't kill them? And I wish I didn't have to lose them either. Though, I'll get my revenge one day. On one, Henri Dupont, the packless who killed them and organised the attacks. He's still out there."

"You'll get him," I reassure Alpha Liam. "And I know my ignorance may annoy you, but what is a packless?"

"Packless are werewolves without a pack. Ones who roam the unclaimed-lands or live among humans like you and your mom did," he explains. "Overall, there are three types of packless. The ones born, the ones banished and the ones that go feral – those types need to be killed, put out of their misery, as they have succumbed to the beast inside us. Not including the ferals, packless despise us, especially Alphas as we represent packs. They believe everyone would be happier packless..."

"I'm sorry for making you talk about them." I lace my fingers with his, as I try to tune out the feeling of his rage and grief that is lashing into our soul bond. "I know it probably isn't the same, but I lost everything once too – the day I met my father for the first time." I pause, swallowing my saliva. I hate him so much. "You know, I've not said his name. It's not like he wants to be my father. Maybe I should just call him by his name, Thomas Blake. Feels weird. Anyway, I lost everything that day. I lost my home, my mum, my human life."

"Your loss is as important as mine," Alpha Liam says, his voice mournful. "This is your home now. You have a home here with me."

Too much emotion overcomes me. I fling myself at Alpha Liam, hugging him harder than I should. If the pained groans are anything to go by.

The idea of home is almost foreign after two years. Burying my face in the crook of his neck, I drink in his scent and listen to the song of his pulse. It would be easy to bite into the soft tender flesh of his throat and guzzle my fill. I bet his blood would be better than anything.

My mouth opens and I allow my teeth to graze his flesh, he shivers. His arms tighten around me. Wordlessly, I know he is giving me permission to bite him, and who am I to refuse? My teeth sink into his throat, his angelic blood dancing into my mouth. His hips buck forward as he moans.

Pushing Alpha Liam against a nearby tree, I know this is right, that no blood will ever satisfy me like his.

"Clay," Alpha Liam moans breathlessly. My whole-body tingles. The moan of my name from his lips is something I believe my body has always craved. "Clay!"

Releasing is a struggle. I have not craved or enjoyed someone's blood as much as this. Untangling my body, I step back, my puncture marks on his throat are already healed. Alpha Liam, my mate, stares at me with hooded eyes. The scent of lust is thick about us. I know if I looked at his crotch, I would see his excitement.

"Do you want to show me your log cabin?" I ask, my voice lower and deeper than normal, whilst I cringe inwardly at the double-entendre. Mutely, he nods, grips my hand and leads me towards the place we will be sleeping. The door is unlocked, rather stupid of him.

The first thing that catches my attention is a desk opposite the door, two chairs on either side and papers covering almost every inch of it. Next, I see a bed pushed against the far wall, animal furs and wool blankets strewn across it and pillows stacked high. My bag is on the mattress.

A bedside table is on either side of the bed, both with stacks of worn looking books. Speaking of books, there are two bookcases full to the brim, standing guard between an open red painted door, revealing a small bathroom and finally, I see a closet, its doors thrown open, I cannot see any bright clothing inside.

"Sorry for the mess," Alpha Liam says awkwardly. Collecting the few dirty articles of clothing on the floor, he then flees into the bathroom to put them into a hamper. When he returns, he heads to his desk to quickly and efficiently stack his papers, which uncovers a purple laptop and a printer hidden by the mess. Once the task is complete, he heads to his closet and shuts the doors. Stuck on the outside of the right door are four photos. Alpha Liam is in each of the photos at different ages. With him are a man, a woman, and two older boys. It doesn't take a genius to know they are his parents and brothers.

The photos hold Alpha Liam's eyes hostage and my soul screams for him. Frowning, I go to my bag and retrieve the photo I hold dear to me. Approaching my mate, I hold it out to him.

His eyes flick to the photo, and he smiles. "You look so happy, so does she. She looks familiar, that's your mom?"

"Mum," I correct. "And yes, that's her. How could she be familiar to you?"

"I think I might know her. What was her name?"

"She called herself Mary Knight – I don't think it was her real name. Why do you need to know?"

"Just give me a second, okay? I think I've seen her before."

He heads to the desk, opens his laptop, photo in hand, and types rapidly. Approaching my mate, I look at his laptop and I am greeted by the younger face of Mum. The bold words above her head reading: *Missing*. And below her face is a name, her real name – Maria Darby.

CHAPTER VIII

Beta JJ called Alpha Liam away, as some packless had attacked the border, leaving me alone with the knowledge that Mum has been considered missing by the Goldstein pack, my ancestral pack, for over eighteen years. All thanks to the database about missing individuals from the Werewolf Council, a worldwide organisation of werewolves who set laws and rules that packs must follow. In simpler terms, they are the werewolf government.

The database also stated that Maria Darby disappeared after rejecting her mate, though her family didn't know why she rejected him. They did not know about me. Did she fear they would reject me like my father? Probably.

I sit on the bed, stopping my pacing. Unlacing my combat boots, I kick them off and submerge myself under the blankets and furs. There was a lot of information about people looking for Mum, false tips and sightings, as well as a report that Father's clan had vanished two years ago.

I also learned that my grandparents died five years ago. I do have living family – my Aunt Hannah. Mum sometimes told me stories of her, but not many, as they seemed to cause her pain. Doesn't she deserve to know what happened to her sister? That she has a nephew? That I'm the reason her sister went into hiding and the reason she died?

Mum's blood is on my hands. If I had not been born, Mum would still be with her sister, her pack and her mate. I know I've thought these thoughts before, but they hurt more than ever. I wish I could talk to Melody. She would have the words, even now, in her weakened state.

"I'm back," Alpha Liam announces and part of me almost weeps with relief. Fleeing the entrapment of the bed, I throw myself at him. His large strong arms perfectly encase me, his fresh scent calms my racing heart. His stale scent in the room and bed had done nothing to help me.

My face is buried in the crook of his neck, his pulse a familiar sound, my fingers gripping the fabric of his tee. This place, this pack, this log cabin, may one day be home, but at the moment, Alpha Liam – no, Liam is home.

I know these feelings and thoughts aren't normal but I can't stop them. It must be the effect of a soul bond as well as my guilt and yearning to be loved, that makes me feel this way.

"I wish I had not needed to leave when you were in such a vulnerable state," Liam, my Liam says.

"It's okay." I lift my head, "I just had a lot to think about. Also, is it strange that my father and his clan are off the Werewolf Council's radar?"

"It is peculiar that their location isn't known. Most clans, like packs, stay in one territory permanently, and your father had claimed that territory for over fifty years," he pauses, thinking. "Plus, I noticed on the document stating their location was unknown, that there was a sentence saying the Werewolf Council had asked the Grand Coven, the magic users' government, if they could locate the clan. However, the request was refused."

Shaking my head, I ask, "Do vampires have a government like the Grand Coven or the Werewolf Council?"

"No, vampires like to follow their own rules. Every clan is different."

"So, no laws about not killing hybrids."

He shakes his head. "Unfortunately, not. It must be hard being hated by him."

"It's not just him," I whisper, pulling away and stepping back from his embrace. "It's everyone. People hate me because I'm a cross-breed. I'm not wolf enough for werewolves and not dead enough for vampires. And I can't change that fact."

"My pack will welcome you; you are already part of the pack; you are Alpha-Male Clay."

"I'm not. I will never truly be welcome," I reveal to him. "Pack members will hate me or whisper to each other that they are pleased we are two men, unable to create a child between us. Speaking of children. How will you get an heir? Will you have to procreate with a woman?"

"That is far off, Clay. And I wouldn't dare cheat on you. We would use a surrogate."

"You yourself said 'odd how genetics work', who's to say you won't need to have half-a-dozen before you get an Alpha babe?"

"Why are we discussing this now? We've known each other for hours; can't we save the heir talk for another time?"

"I don't know. The idea of you having a child with someone hurts." I place my hand on my chest. "My heart breaks at the idea."

"I suppose if you had a child with someone else, I would feel a little crazy too. However, this is way off in the distant future. Plus, an Alpha child may be born in my pack and they could become my heir."

Frowning, I am shocked I just acted that possessive. "I can't believe I started this heated discussion in under four hours of knowing you."

"It's normal," Liam assures me. "The soul bond forces our emotions to develop faster than normal. Because I literally told you within an hour of meeting you that I would protect you until my dying day, and that you were my family, my blood and my heart. If that isn't coming on strong, I don't know what is."

I laugh happily. "I liked it."

I close the distance between us and snog him, my arms wrapping around his neck. His arms go around my waist, our tongues battling. We're alone in a room with a bed, maybe we should – no, not yet, there is no need to rush.

"You are a good kisser," Liam mumbles, taking deep breaths to recover. "I know this might seem random – but do you want to go on a run with me?"

My heart plummets and I see Mum's face, full of disappointment and sorrow. How will Liam react? Like Mum? Will he pretend it doesn't affect him, doesn't upset him, doesn't ruin some childhood dream?

"I can't..." I begin, trailing off, not able to tell him.

"You can't what? You can tell me anything."

"What if it makes you no longer want me?"

"There is nothing that could do that," he confidently states.

I almost want to scoff at the idiocy of the statement. Still, I speak, not able to look into his eyes. "I can't shift. On my twelfth birthday, I didn't change when all werewolves do. I don't have a wolf form, not like a pureblood werewolf. The most I can do is half-shift, changing my nails into claws, that is the extent of my shifting abilities."

"Look at me," Liam orders and I obey. "I don't care if you can shift or not. I thought you might not, but that doesn't change anything. Maybe tomorrow we can run together, me in wolf form and you trying to keep up."

I laugh. "I think you'll find I'm faster, Alpha-boy."

"Alpha-boy? I like it." He grins, and I feel myself become dumb at that smile. "We'll discover who's the best then. I'm going to get us dinner. Do you need blood?"

"No, I only need to feed every two days."

"Good to know. I look forward to you biting me again."

I flush and watch him exit, thinking of his body pressed against mine, his hips bucking forwards and my name escaping his lips. I can't wait for my next feeding either.

. . .

Liam is back in five minutes; the food is amazing. We eat at his desk, telling stories of our lives. I'm careful not to mention my time on the streets. I'm sure Alpha Andrew told him I was homeless; however, those are days best forgotten. The cold nights, the crimes I committed to survive, and the fight over food, shelter and money with humans far weaker than me.

"We should get ready for bed," Liam says, getting up and retrieving a pair of flannel pyjamas from his closet to give to me.

Thanking him, I excuse myself into the bathroom, leaving behind my sunglasses on Liam's desk. Pulling on my borrowed pyjamas, I look into the mirror, my freaky mutated eyes staring back at me, as I assess the ridiculousness of my borrowed flannel pyjamas on my frame. For I've had to tie the pyjama bottom's drawstring extremely tight to keep them up. I've always been scrawny, no one would suspect I would have the strength to lift a car or throw a person across a room.

Running my fingers through my hair, I gather the strands and use an elastic band to put my hair in a man-bun. *You look ugly,* the voice in my head snarls. *Do you think he really finds an abomination like you attractive? He just doesn't want to reject you. His pack would frown upon him, breaking a soul bond is sacrilegious to werewolf culture, like spitting in the face of their Goddess.*

Yanking the elastic band out of my hair, I collapse to the ground and fight the urge not to descend into a sobbing mess. How can I know he really wants me? *He let you feed from him and said he looked forward to next time,* a kinder voice in my head reminds me. *He promised to protect you when it will bring danger to his pack. He cares for you.*

Groaning, I wonder why life couldn't be simple like it was when I pretended to be human. Those sixteen years were bliss.

Speedily, I brush my teeth. Upon finishing the task, I place my toothbrush next to Liam's, and a small smile spreads on my face at seeing them together. I have someone now to hold me. Exiting the bathroom, I see Liam is already on the bed, lying over the blankets and furs in a pair of black boxers. My face grows hot seeing my soulmate's almost naked body. Liam is all muscles, defined pecs, abs to die for, very muscular legs and arms, he's any bodybuilder's wet dream.

"I get hot," he states anxiously. "I only wear pyjamas when it is really cold, but I can wear them if it makes you feel more comfortable?"

"It's okay," I say, feeling the heat rise to my face. "Sleep in whatever you want." I get into bed, slipping under the wool blankets and heavy animal furs. "Did you hunt and skin the animals yourself?"

"No, some were hunted and skinned by my parents, others by my brothers."

I sense his grief through our bond and press against him, wrapping an arm around his very toned stomach, as I rest my head on his defined pecs. He is all muscle, all man, all Alpha, and he's mine. And what does he get? A scrawny abomination.

I look up at Liam, his stormy grey eyes meeting mine. "Do you find me attractive, Liam?"

"Of course," he replies, without hesitation. "You are gorgeous."

Still, it does nothing to ease the knot in my stomach. I'm not good enough. He's an Alpha. I'm a freak. He's muscular. I'm scrawny. He could have anyone he wants. So, then why me? Why did destiny, or the Goddess, pair us together? We have good chemistry though, there is no doubting that.

"You can tell me anything," Liam whispers, one of his calloused hands rubbing my back. "I promise."

Shame bubbles in my stomach as I realise, he must be feeling my insecurity through our soul bond. Curse that thing. Sighing, I roll away from him and hug myself. The bed shifts as Liam slips under the blankets and furs, his hard muscles and warm flesh, soon pushing against me.

"JJ's mate Tegan, she's human," Liam says suddenly. I raise my eyebrows and roll over to face him. Humans and supernaturals don't normally mix well, or so I'm told. "She's a rare human who can see the supernatural, she figured out what we were when she was only six. By doing so, she learned to stay away from the werewolves that attended her school. Although, unlike most of my pack, I didn't go to the school in Lockborough, I was home-schooled. But that's deviating from the point of the story. Anyway, Tegan always had a wariness about the supernatural so when she bumped into JJ, she was insecure, nervous and fearful towards him. JJ probably should have used his brain because he stupidly outed himself as her soulmate, right in the middle of the street. Tegan was confused and must have misunderstood something he said, because she thought JJ meant her harm, so she ran and JJ followed. She made it home, got her father's gun and when JJ broke in, she shot him. My point being, if you are feeling insecure or fearful or confused, don't grab a gun and shoot me, let's just talk. So, why were you feeling insecure, fearful and confused? How you look? Because you are gorgeous, Clay. Believe me when I say that."

"I believe you," I lie, but I know he doesn't. In a quick fluid motion, he straddles me, his arse pressing against my crotch. My breath hitches, his stormy grey eyes glare down at me, his strong powerful body looming over me, his calloused hands cupping my face.

"I've dreamed of you since I was a boy and if you ask anyone, you'll find that I don't lie to those I care about. So, when I say someone is gorgeous, I mean it, I fucking mean it."

My mouth is as dry as a desert, a fog descending over my mind. Nervously, I flick my tongue over my bottom lip.

Liam leans downwards, his breath wafting over my face. "Was that an invitation to kiss you?"

Gulping, I nod and his hot moist mouth is against mine. There is no battle of dominance this time, he is in charge. His calloused hands trail down my body, slowly unbuttoning my borrowed flannel pyjama top.

I'm powerless under him and I love it.

His hands explore my naked torso, memorising the contours. The skilled lips migrate away from my mouth, sucking and nipping at my neck, forming what I can only imagine will be colourful fleeting hickeys, as my healing will erase the evidence.

Abruptly I moan embarrassingly loud as he begins tweaking my already hard nipples. A soft chuckle comes out of his mouth at finding a sensitive part of my body. He's learning how to make me feel good, making my heart swells.

Liam is kissing me again, my moans vibrating against his lips, as his fingers continue their onslaught. One hand halts its work and grazes my privates, snapping me to my senses.

"Stop," I whisper, "we should stop, we have time."

His lips and hands stop their work and a petulant whine exits my lips. How I wish I had not spoken. My body feels charged and starved, so very starved for his skilled hands and lips.

"You are right, we have our whole lives in front of us. So, if you wouldn't mind, I need a cold shower."

Liam climbs off me and stumbles into the bathroom, the door closing behind him, shortly followed by the sound of running water. Maybe I should have a shower too. My body continues feeling exhilarated and ravenous in a way it has never been. Not even with Sabrina, whom I lost my virginity to and she was very skilled.

Sometimes, I think about her, she was an interesting woman. No, she was a girl, she wasn't a woman.

We were sixteen and pretty much innocent. Sabrina always wanted to see my eyes. I did not cave and my eyes remained a mystery to her. I would not subject her to a death vision.

I hope she is well and has found love. For while I can't say I love Liam, I know it will happen soon.

As we are soulmates, our relationship is for life.

Buttoning my pyjama top back up, I roll onto my side and shut my eyes. Minutes go by before the shower stops running and a few more until the bed shifts with Liam's weight. Quickly followed by his arms around me.

Smiling, I allow sleep to invade my mind, dragging me into the abyss.

CHAPTER IX

I gain consciousness to the sound of tapping. Peeling my eyelids open, I see Liam at his desk typing away at his laptop. The scent of Beta JJ is faint, he was here recently, while I slept. My stomach clenches, I should have woken. My instincts should have woken me. What if Beta JJ was a threat? I could have been killed in my sleep. Sitting up, I anxiously run my fingers through my hair.

Liam stops typing and looks at me, stormy grey eyes full of worry. "I feel your distress. Are you okay?"

"No," I answer. "When was Beta JJ here?"

"Just call him JJ and he was here ten or twenty minutes ago. Why?"

"I should have woken up upon his intrusion."

"JJ is harmless."

"No one is harmless – I was vulnerable," I snap, sounding like a hysterical child.

"If that's how you feel, then I won't let anyone come in while you are asleep."

"That's how I feel, Alpha-boy. I should have woken up when he came, I should have woken up."

"Hey," Liam says, leaving his desk and coming to my side. His rough hands cupping my face. "Everything is going to be okay. I was here to protect you."

"What if you weren't here? What if I was asleep and someone came in, someone my father paid to kill me. It wouldn't be the first time."

"The first time?" he questions. "What do you mean by that?"

I sigh and lie back down onto the mattress; I hate how stupid I was. "In the beginning, my father and his clan didn't actively chase me. They sent others after me. I think they thought it was easier than wasting their time on me. Nevertheless, after six months of failure, my father decided he and his clan would be the ones to deal with me."

Briefly, I am lost to the past. "In those six months, I dealt with werewolves, vampires, and even one witch, who decided to come after me with relative ease. I moved faster than them, and could knock anyone out with a single blow. However, I was unprepared for the first one. It had been two weeks since I fled from my home, leaving Mum to die. I was grieving, not hardened or skilled to a life on the streets." I had been such a fool. "When I saw Johnny, I knew he was a vampire instantly. He didn't bother to hide his red eyes or his scent. I went to run; I was going to run."

"What happened?" Liam demands, his sorrow and anger resonating both in his voice and our soul bond. "What did he do?"

"He didn't do anything then; he had a loaf of bread and he offered it to me. I had taught myself to feed off humans and how to compel them to forget, two things I had never done two weeks prior. Though I may have quenched my thirst, I had not consumed human food in over a week, and that loaf of bread looked like something worth dying for. Every day, for the next three weeks, we would meet and Johnny would give me food, money and tips on feeding on the living. I'm ashamed to admit, I trusted him. So, when Johnny asked if I wanted to go with him to his hotel room, I didn't hesitate. I think, looking back, I had developed a crush on him. He was rather handsome and was stuck eternally at the age of eighteen."

Liam growls, a furious primal sound. Sitting up, I see Liam on his knees, his nails replaced with claws, eyes luminous red, a thin layer of pitch-black fur covering his skin. I had never seen a werewolf close to an accidental transformation.

"I can stop. I don't need to finish."

"No," Liam snarls, his voice more beast than man, "finish it."

"Okay," I reply anxiously. "At the hotel room, I took a shower, ate food and we – drank from a human together. Then, I went to sleep. It was a deep sleep, a type of sleep I should not have awoken from. Except, I did and I woke to the feeling of his hands on my throat, trying to rip my head off my body," I shiver at the memory. "I hadn't slept with my sunglasses on, so when my eyes opened, Johnny had a vision of his death. He paled, stepped away and told me why he tried to end my life. Turns out dear old Father was paying half a million for my head. And Johnny figured the best way to kill an abomination like me was to gain my trust, then attempt to kill me. Once he finished his confession, I punched him in the face. He flew across the room and through the wall to the outside. I don't think Johnny was a daywalker, as we didn't meet in the daytime, nor do I think he woke up before the sun rose. So, I think he died."

Liam has managed to take control of his emotions and is back to looking like his normal human self, well, a sad normal human. Tears fill his stormy grey eyes. Pushing off the bed, I join him on the floor. One of his calloused hands reaches out to touch my face. "I won't let anyone in here if you are asleep, I swear it on the Goddess. It must have been so hard to live like you did, for the last two years."

"It was. I did things I would like to forget. Leaving Johnny to the sun is one of those things that I best not remember."

"He deserved it!"

"Johnny just wanted the money. That was his sin: greed. All it takes is one person being greedy."

"No one in my pack would do that. No one would betray me by trying to kill you."

"Are you a hundred percent sure, Alpha-boy?" I reason.

"No – I wish I could, yet I'm not. I pay them well, everyone has a job and gets paid for that, be it pack warrior, cook, cleaner or doctor, although I don't pay half-million. I can imagine a lot of my pack members would take that money and do anything that person asked."

Greed consumes everyone.

"How do you make money to pay everyone?" I ask, changing the subject. "It's not like you work a job. Do you like, invest or something?"

He chuckles, a small smile on his lips. My heart is glad that I have steered the conversation away from Johnny and my father.

"I do invest and sometimes gamble in the stock market, though Willow pack's main income is the businesses we own. Managing all that is about sixty percent of what I do in a day."

"Sounds hard work."

"It is. Luckily, my parents trained me how to do all that stuff since I could talk. If they hadn't, let's just say we would be hugely broke." My stomach gurgles and Liam laughs. "I guess we should get breakfast. I think I should have enough time, before combat training. As, everyday either JJ or me runs it, afterwards I will be free to go on our run."

I grin. "I'm going to beat you, Alpha-boy."

"Oh, yeah, race you to pack house."

"Can't wait then?"

"Nope."

"Just let me get my sunglasses."

He nods and watches as I walk over to his desk to collect my sunglasses. Once placing them on my face, I realise how strange it is. I just had a whole conversation without them on.

"You ready?" he questions, standing and bouncing on the heels of his feet.

"I was born ready."

"On your mark, get ready, GO!" We both race towards the door, smiling. Reaching the door first, I fling it open and I rush outside into the morning sunlight.

Much to Liam's embarrassment, I win. Nevertheless, a smile remains on his face as we enter the pack house.

It's the first time I have been inside this pack house. I follow Liam through unfamiliar rooms and halls, pack members greeting us with loud *hellos,* wide smiles and *nice to see you Alpha-Male Clay.* It is when we reach one of the many pack house's kitchens that I realise I am still in the borrowed pyjamas. Flushing red, I wish the ground would swallow me whole.

"I think you look cute in them," Liam says with a smirk.

I want to curse the bugger as he's fully dressed in a dark blue tee, jeans and black trainers, whilst I'm in these ridiculous oversized flannel pyjamas. The pack members in the kitchen chuckle, even the cooks who are busy trying not to burn the assortment of food.

Liam collects two plates and cutlery, both of which were displayed in large quantities on the kitchen island. Within seconds, one of the cooks' rushes to put pancakes and bacon onto our plates, ignoring the seven pack members waiting for their plates to be filled. Perks of being Alpha and the Alpha-Male, I suppose.

Once our plates are sufficiently filled, Liam leads me out of the kitchen and back the way we came. Heading back to the privacy of our log cabin is something I am thankful for. I don't think I would have managed to eat in front of everyone. They all seem too friendly, *smiling* too happily at me and greeting me as if we were old friends. Shaking those thoughts away, I sigh with relief upon stepping out of the pack house. Enjoying the frigid morning air.

"I know that must have been overwhelming," Liam states as we meander back to the log cabin. "A pack is like a family, we care for our own, even if we don't know each other well."

I nod, opening the log cabin door for Liam. Once inside, we go to his desk, him sitting on one side, me on the other. Liam puts the plate with the more generous helping in front of me, then hands me a knife and fork. We finish our food very quickly; I would say we bring new meaning to people who wolf down their food. I laugh out loud at my own joke, making Liam quirk an eyebrow in confusion. "I'm going to go now. Set a few things up. You don't need to come if you don't want to."

"I'll come later; I have to see my big strong Alpha-boy in action, don't I?"

Liam blushes and stands, puffing out his chest proudly. "You will give me an ego if you keep that up."

Smiling, I observe him leave, causing something in my chest to ache. For goodness' sake, get a grip, he isn't even that far away. Standing, I move about grabbing a red tee, some clean underwear, a pair of jog bottoms and my combat boots.

Then I saunter into the bathroom, place the clothing and combat boots on the closed toilet seat and shut the door. Next, I remove my borrowed flannel pyjamas and sunglasses. Now naked, I switch on the shower and step under the cold spray.

Absentmindedly, I take in the bathroom, it is quite small and simple with only a toilet, a shower cubicle, a hamper, a hanging rack with towels and a sink with a mirror above it.

Cleaning myself using Liam's shampoo, a possessive part of me preens at the idea of smelling like him.

Once I decide I've cleaned myself sufficiently, I switch the shower off, dry myself using a towel. Then dress in my clothes, put on my combat boots, place my sunglasses on and tie my wet hair into a man-bun.

Hurriedly I brush my teeth, my heart yearning to see Liam. Spitting out the toothpaste, I put my toothbrush next to Liam's and leave the bathroom.

The morning has warmed up a fraction when I stroll outside. A small smile graces my lips at the idea of seeing Liam again. Gosh, this soul bond is practically making me co-dependant. I can hear Liam's voice, his lovely voice. It sounds strange and I find myself increasing my pace like a dog rushing to meet its master.

The training ground is a large tarmac square, as large and long as the pack house. One end has a wooden obstacle course, on another side is exercise equipment and weights. Liam stands in the middle of the space talking to someone angrily – a stunning man. His face is angular, cheekbones defined, a light stubble on his cheeks, curly shoulder-length blonde hair, captivating sky-blue eyes and he's dressed, in a grey jumper, taunt over his muscular torso, tight blue jog bottoms and expensive-looking trainers – he looks like a model.

"I told you, Victor, it's over!" Liam shouts. "It has been over for a while."

"I don't care," the model replies, his voice sensual. "I know you feel what I feel!"

"I care for you, I always will, despite what you did. But Clay is my soulmate. Now stop, people are going to start arriving."

"Don't want them to see us together?"

"No, I don't. It's over."

Liam turns to move away; however, Victor spins him back around and slams his lips onto his. Liam doesn't pull away. My heart wails. I flinch as someone takes my hand and tugs me forwards. Without resistance, I follow whoever is leading me away, leading me into the woods.

Slowly, very slowly, my senses return to me and I understand that Victor is Liam's ex. That before Liam got me, a scrawny abomination, he got Victor, who could be acting in movies, commercials and taking part in fashion shows. Why would Liam want me over Victor?

"Sit," an authoritative voice, demands. I obey, dropping onto the ground, in the middle of a meadow full of wildflowers. How long of a walk was it here?

I can't seem to remember. A woman plops down next to me, clad in jeans, a zipped-up leather jacket and knee-length boots.

"I wonder," she begins, "when he's going to realise that's he majorly fucked up?"

We sit in silence; I can't muster a reply. Liam didn't kiss Victor willingly, nor did he pull away and neither, did we hear him shout as we left. So, they must have been still kissing. And if Liam did care about me, he would have felt my jealousy, confusion and pain through the soul bond. Maybe he didn't notice, or worse, he felt it and didn't care. Either way, he's fucked up as this woman suggested.

"I'm Tegan FYI, I'm sure you've heard of me, I'm rather infamous!"

"You shot JJ," I deadpan, my heart continuing to wail.

"Yep, everyone loves that story. Nevertheless, it's JJ's fault – he shouldn't have blurted everything out. I thought he was going to kidnap me or eat me or something. Though that story is irrelevant here," she says dismissively. "Anyhow, before I was with JJ, I had a few girlfriends and boyfriends. One of my boyfriends, I can't remember his name, kissed another girl while we were together, so I didn't speak to him for a month. And we ended up staying together for a year."

"I'm not sure what that situation has to do with it?" I scoff rudely. "Your former boyfriend isn't your soulmate? So, it's not the same."

"I wasn't saying the situations were similar," she snorts. "I am suggesting you don't talk to Alpha Liam for a month, as punishment, or you could just punch him in the dick, that's always fun to do."

I raise my eyebrows and look at Tegan. She's a desirable woman with close cropped black hair, chocolate brown eyes, olive skin and multiple piercings in her ears. Danger seems to come off her in waves. She's the type of person I would expect to carry a weapon on her person.

"Dick punching does seem fun," I respond vengefully.

"Then let's go back there and punch Alpha Liam's dick, I hear it's big. Have you seen it?"

I flush. "No, I haven't."

"Boo, you should fix that once he's been punished."

"But is dick punching really the solution?" I ponder. "We're meant to be soulmates, and within twenty-four hours – he's cheated!"

"In all seriousness, Victor and him were together for a year, and they only broke up two months ago," Tegan says. "Maybe, Alpha Liam might have seen the kiss as a goodbye. So, don't write him off. Alpha Liam's a good guy, sometimes an idiot – a lot of men are."

"Ouch, I am offended for all mankind."

"I didn't say all, you seem alright, Clay."

"Thanks, I guess. But why did they break up?" I question.

"Victor cheated," Tegan states. "It really hurt Alpha Liam; they were best friends before they got together. And were inseparable since Victor and his mother moved to Willow pack when he was eight," she pauses and frowns. "The whole pack continues to be furious towards Victor for what he did. We are all very happy you are here Clay."

Her last sentence makes me feel very warm. Pushing it aside, I realise something. "Why do you call me Clay and not Alpha-Male Clay?"

"Because I hate being called Beta-Female Tegan and I thought, you might dislike titles too. As you were raised among humans like me. And FYI, your story is public knowledge, gossip and secrets spread like wildfire in a pack. Plus, even if it didn't, everyone wants to know about the cute hybrid, which Alpha Liam is soul bonded to."

"Cute?" I huff in annoyance. "I'm not cute."

"That's not what most of the pack thinks," Tegan chuckles. "I mean those oversized flannel pyjamas totally added to your cute factor."

My face burns like a dozen suns. "You saw that?"

"I think the whole pack did. We were all curious about you and can already tell how happy Liam and you make each other." She pauses, considering something. "He's been a bit down since the breakup with Victor. It has been horrible to see."

My heart twists at the thought of Liam being depressed. "You really think it was a goodbye kiss?" I whisper, feeling so very vulnerable.

"I do and I believe, Liam would have told you afterwards if you had not witnessed it," Tegan says confidently. "He's going to feel like the king of idiots when he realises you were there."

"You've convinced me on that," I admit. "Nor am I jealous or angry with him anymore."

"Good," Tegan smiles, then abruptly her face morphs into a different expression. "Does that mean he doesn't get a dick punch?"

I laugh. The way Tegan's face fell was hilarious. "No, there will be a dick punching."

"Hooray! Can I be there? Please let me be there."

"I don't think I could stop you."

"Agreed," Tegan replies eagerly, "nothing could stop me."

"I think we will be fast friends."

Snorting, she smiles. "Clay, consider me your friend already, because we are in the same boat. Despite what our soulmates may say, we will always be the outcasts of this place. I'm a human and you are a hybrid in a pack of werewolves. We will never truly belong."

"No, no we won't," I agree. "Though, at least all you have to do is go to Lockborough to find your own people. I have none. For I've never heard of or seen another hybrid. And if there is, they won't be like me – they won't have my eyes."

"You forget, I'm a human who can see the supernatural. I've lied about the things I've seen, since my parents got scared, about the 'stories' I was making up." She shivers in dramatic horror. "And like you – I've never met another human who sees what I do."

"That does sound as lonely as my existence."

"Probably not as lonely. You are half-vampire, aren't you?"

"Yeah, why?"

"Have you really not realised what that could mean for your future?"

I shake my head in confusion. "What do you mean?"

"Vampires are immortal – you could be too."

CHAPTER X

Tegan strolled back to the training ground with me. It took seven minutes, during which I realised how moronic I am. In my eighteen years, I had not considered I might be immortal. It's not like it's a secret that vampires are immortal! I could still be alive in a century or an aeon. I could see cities rise and nations fall. Yet the worse thing about my possible immortality is that I will be alone – everyone I know and care about will be dead.

Upon arriving at the training ground, combat training is in full swing. Half-shifted men and women are sparring, their Delta or Gamma eyes out to play. There are also fully-shifted pack members in wolf form. Lunging and biting one another, their werewolves' eyes shining proudly. Additionally, there is a few pack members scaling the obstacle course, while some are lifting weights.

My eyes are naturally drawn to Liam, he's shirtless, his abs glistening, half-shifted, sparring against five fully-shifted pack members, his claws soaked in blood. Looking away, I spot others observing the combat training with varying degrees of expression, their Delta or Omega eyes shining with powerful emotion. It seems combat training is a popular thing to watch.

Usurpingly, Tegan is staring at JJ whose eyes are shining

luminous purple, as he is fighting against two half-shifted delta women with a metal staff. JJ is a very skilled fighter, something his skinny, lean appearance would not point to. His stature is not completely unique among the swarm of sparring and training pack members, though they seem to be the minority. Most werewolves seem muscular, even females. Could be genetic – Mum had muscular arms.

"I'm going to lie down," I inform Tegan, absently.

She inclines her head, licking her lips as JJ yanks his top off, revealing a toned stomach and a lot of chest hair. If she had been a werewolf, her eyes would be glowing like the others. Trekking to the log cabin, I ponder if I will stop ageing soon or if I will start to age slower.

Shaking the nagging immortality thoughts away, I push open the log cabin door and freeze. On our bed, the bed we had slept on the night before – is Victor.

"In person, you are even less unimpressive." Victor smiles cruelly. "No muscles, something Liam always loved about me. He used to grip my arms as he made love to me. For that is what we have – love. Tell me, has he fucked you? Did he call out my name? Or hasn't he touched you because the mere sight of your scrawny half-breed body repulses you?" His words feel like punches, my knees beg to give out. "I know you saw us kiss. I could hear your heart shattering. He may refute it; however, he loves me, he always will. I was his first, you do not forget your first." A true statement, I will always remember Sabrina. "When we were younger, we used to tell each other horror stories about hybrids. We were both, disgusted at their mere existence. I bet he continues to feel the same way. So, do everyone a favour and reject him." Victor leaps out of the bed and approaches me. "You don't deserve to be the Alpha-Male and once I am his chosen mate, I'll make sure Tegan and JJ get demoted. No human should be Beta-Female. And no one except pureblood werewolves should be in a pack. Don't you think?"

Victor waits for my reply, I don't know why. He doesn't actually want an answer. The cruel smile is still on his face. I don't know how

Liam could even tolerate this person. He's clearly a pureblood extremist like my father. Biting my bottom lip, I picture Tegan holding JJ, as Liam tells the two that JJ will no longer be his Beta. It boils my blood.

My hands shake, my nails grow into claws and my eyesight, sharpens in a way it has not done before. I see something in his human sky-blue eyes, I see his werewolf eyes. And they are silver. I don't know how I can see beyond his human eyes, or how I know for certain he is a sacred werewolf like Melody. Then I remember what Melody told me.

"Those who look upon your eyes see their death, it changes people, and you have more talents, talents best learnt by yourself."

This is one of my hidden talents, to look past the human eyes of werewolves and see their second eyes. Somehow, I sense this is a secret, that no one knows about him being gifted by the Goddess.

"Are you mentally challenged or something?" Victor demands.

"No, I was just thinking," I answer swiftly. "And I disagree with your statement that a pack should be for purebloods only. That's some backwards thinking." Pausing, I decide to ask him a question, knowing it will anger him. He seems the type to be upset at suggesting he's subservient and submissive. "I know this might insult you, but – are you an Omega?"

His eyes don't flash luminous silver, his eyes remain their human sky-blue, though fury is borne on his face, at me questioning if he is an Omega. "I'm a Delta werewolf."

"Then show me. Show me your orange eyes."

He tilts his head to the side and frowns. "You know, don't you? A secret I kept my entire life and you, just know?"

"How did you hide it?"

"I have impeccable self-control," he brags, "and no one ever suspected I was lying. How come an abomination like you knows?"

"Because I see your eyes, your werewolf eyes, hiding behind your human ones. Why keep it a secret?"

"Many reasons. One being, I would have to register myself with the Werewolf Council as a sacred werewolf, something my parents' thought was best kept hidden." Victor leans close to me, his arm pushing past me, slamming the door shut, the expression on his face serious. "I can't let you tell anyone, Clay. Killing you will mean I'll have to run and break Liam's little heart. However, Willow pack has been a bit of a drag for the last two months."

"That's your fault," I gulp. "You shouldn't have cheated."

"What can I say? He was a smoking hot human and he wasn't the first man, I banged outside our relationship. Now as I'm going to kill you, I can tell you this, for I know it will hurt you," his eyes transform to luminous silver, like liquid moonlight. "I was the one who shot Melody."

CHAPTER XI

My body goes numb, and I'm back in the meadow, holding Melody as she bleeds out. Her attempted killer is here, right in front of me, leaning in close. A calloused hand, a hand similar to Liam's, touches my cheek tenderly, a cruel smile once more on his face.

"Once you are dead," Victor states, "I'm going to see Melody. I think she's suffered enough without her Sight."

"How do you know she lost her Sight?" I whisper, wondering if I'm strong enough to take on a sacred werewolf. I don't think I am. What gift could Victor have that rivals the ability to see the future, past and present?

"Because I laced the bullets with wolfsbane and once it enters the bloodstream, it represses our blessing," he explains condescendingly. "It could take days, weeks, or even years for her to regain her gift. And her gift is the only thing Melody has ever known and had. Without it, she is nothing."

"You sound like you know her?"

He chuckles. "Biding time aren't you, Clay? Sadly, this will be the last reveal."

"I'm not scared to die," I say, trying to be brave. "I'm scared to live."

"I won't spare you if that is why you said that?"

"No, I'm genuinely scared to live. I could be immortal."

"Hmm," Victor hums, both of his callous hands going onto my face, "sad that you'll never find out."

I gulp. "Tell me then, tell me how you know Melody?"

"Fine," he sighs. "I don't know her personally, my father did, Alpha Drake Shadow, of Shadow pack," Victor informs me, and I tense. Alpha Drake was Melody's kidnapper. "I was conceived in a one-night stand. While he knew of my existence, he could not raise me. I would be a weakness, so he made my mother leave and raise me alone. We moved about a lot and eventually settled in Willow pack; Father visited on occasion. On my ninth birthday, Father told me of the seer he had taken. A girl who could see the future. Except, she couldn't see me. I don't think she can see others like us. So, she did not know of my existence.

In Father's care, he used Melody to make Shadow pack the strongest in America. While I lived here, no one discovering my relationship to Alpha Drake or that I was a sacred werewolf." Victor's grip on my face tightens. "Until you just looked at me a few minutes ago and knew my true status."

My heart pounds. He will kill me. I need a way to survive, think Clay! "Why did you try to kill Melody?"

"Stop stalling and weren't you listening earlier? I shot her to render her powerless, not to kill her. Stage two is killing her. As Melody had to suffer first, for killing my father and destroying what remained of my ancestral pack." A vicious growl bursts from his lips. "I never believed she died, and I was right. She didn't keep a low profile, so it was easy to keep tabs on her. And I waited for her to return and she did. Now, no more talk, it is time you die."

"No, no I won't be dying," I put my plan into motion, well, an action. Curling my right hand into a ball, I punch Victor in the dick. Thank you for the advice, Tegan. He collapses onto the ground, making a very unmanly sound, his hands cradling his crotch.

Spinning around, I fling the door open and run outside. I make about ten steps when searing pain erupts throughout my body, my vision going black. A sound fills my ears. It takes a second to understand it is my own scream.

By the time my vision returns, a crowd has gathered. An audience to my death. Some pack members must have tried to help me, as they lie unconscious on the ground.

Liam is close to an accidental transformation again. His skin covered in a thick layer of fur, his red eyes blazing like an inferno, his blooded claws ready to attack. JJ, the dutiful Beta, is holding him back. Tegan is next to them, holding JJ's metal staff.

"I wanted to sneak away, Clay!" I gasp in pain as a powerful-kick slams into my gut. "Now everyone knows I'm a sacred werewolf." Victor stands over me, his eyes still liquid moonlight, a furious expression on his face. "The single plus to the spectacle, you have made is that I get to kill you in front of Liam."

"I'll fucking end you!" Liam snarls, bones snapping as the shifting begins. "There won't be anything left of you to bury. That is a promise."

"I love your dirty talk, baby." Victor chuckles. "Unfortunately, you won't get the chance. I can just render you unconscious like the idiots before you," he gestures to the knocked-out forms of a handful of pack members. "So, baby, stop shifting. I'll just make you a sleeping wolf."

Liam doesn't take his advice. I observe with morbid fascination as his body contorts, bones snapping and reshaping, his face elongating, his teeth becoming too big for his human mouth, his clothing, ripped to shreds in the process. Within seconds, JJ is trying his best to hold back a car-sized, black-furred wolf, with teeth like razor-sharp daggers and glimmering red eyes, that ominously glare at Victor.

I can understand why Mum would not let me watch her shift, it is a horrifying process. Liam's wolf form could invoke fear to any sane person. Victor, though, is not sane and simply smiles, as if Liam is a cute little Chihuahua. "Don't you look adorable, Liam?"

Liam howls. The sound curdles my blood and JJ releases him. The pain that had been erupting in my body stops and my screams go with it. Victor's smile has fallen. Liam and the audience, including Tegan and JJ charge. Victor will meet his maker.

Unfortunately, that does not happen. About two feet away, every one of them drops to the ground, howling and wailing in agony. The cause is obvious: Victor. He can inflict pain on others. Why would the Goddess bless someone with that ability?

I need to stop him. Forcing my numb limbs, I yank my sunglasses off and weakly lunge at Victor, tackling his legs out from under him. Snarling, his liquid moonlight eyes gaze down at me and I see what he sees. Victor sees his death, and I have a role in it.

He is on his back, choking on his own blood, and I stand over him. I look different. My hair is cut in a military style, my skin somehow is sun-kissed. I've never been able to get any colour in my vampiric skin. Both my arms have gained muscle, but the most shocking thing is my eyes. They are not my own. The pupils are black and circular, the sclerae white, both human-like. However, my irises are golden and blaze like a thousand suns at midday.

"Your time is over," my future-self utters, unnatural power vibrating out of his voice. I can't make out the clothing I wear or the location his death will take place. "You lost, and no one will mourn you."

"Fuck... you," Victor chokes out, blood dribbling down his lips, like the blood that had dribbled out of Melody's mouth in the meadow. "Fuck you all."

My future-self smiles, a cruel smile, the type of smile Victor was giving me earlier. "If that's how you feel, you can die alone."

Returning to the present, I'm still on his legs, shakily, I stand. Victor doing the same. I take a step toward him and he takes a step back.

"I'm fated to kill you," I deadpan. "And nothing can change that."

I'm not sure if that's certain, I can't be, not like if it was Melody predicting the future. Victor doesn't know that. And like the coward he is, Victor runs into the woods, his body shifting and changing into his wolf form. His clothes shredded into nothing.

I could catch him, yet there could be a chance he would snap out of his fear and start using his pain infliction gift again. So, I will wait until next time, and there will be a next time, I feel it in my gut.

It took twenty minutes for everyone to awaken from their pain-induced unconsciousness. Then I explained everything that happened and what Victor revealed to me – his heritage, his bigotry and his gift. Once I finish, Liam tries to pull me aside so we can talk. I refuse and tell him we would talk about everything later. JJ then whisked him away so they could begin making their calls to Reed pack and the Werewolf Council.

I couldn't talk to Liam; I needed time to think. Liam literally dated and fucked a literal psycho, who I'm fated to kill.

Although I didn't spend the rest of the day alone, I spent it with Tegan, who showed me around the pack house and introduced me to pack members. The latter taking most of the time up.

The sun has set when I arrive at the log cabin door. I can hear Liam discussing with JJ about the threat of the packless. There was another attack three hours ago, luckily no one died. Still, whatever the threat the packless may pose, it is nothing compared against Victor – he is a gigantic threat.

For he took out every pack warrior who wasn't patrolling the border at the time. All of them taken out in a blink of an eye. And the only reason they survived is because of my freaky mutated eyes. Eyes that somehow showed the future to me as well as him and will somehow be different in the future.

Pushing the door open, JJ and Liam flinch. I ignore both and stroll into the bathroom. Locking the door behind me, I change into my borrowed flannel pyjamas and brush my teeth. Upon the two tasks being finished, I exit the bathroom. Liam is alone and sits on the bed in his boxers. Tension is thick.

Part of my mind remembers Victor had been lying down where I will be sleeping, that Liam must have screwed Victor in our bed, that maybe an hour before Victor tried to kill me, Liam had his lips on his. Can we get past this?

"We've warned Reed pack about Victor," Liam says awkwardly. "Alpha Andrew said Melody's doing well. I'm sure she will be happy to know who the shooter was."

"Yeah, I'm sure she's pleased to know her kidnapper's son is out for revenge," I snap back at him. "That her abilities were suppressed using wolfsbane. I mean, what's next? Finding out silver, really is deadly towards her."

"It is," Liam states tensely, "the Werewolf Council informed me that sacred werewolves are allergic to silver and wolfsbane, really does repress their gifts. We couldn't just believe Victor," I scoff, he would not lie, he thought he was speaking to a dead man. "The information is something the Werewolf Council has kept hidden for centuries. Though, silver and wolfsbane on non-sacred werewolves is harmless."

I fight the urge to growl. "I know that wolfsbane and silver are harmless to normal werewolves," I say, annoyed that he thought I didn't know. "My mum told me that many things' humans came up with about the supernatural were a myth. For example, vampires aren't allergic to holy water and can enter holy places."

"Sorry." He flushes. "I didn't mean to imply you were ignorant."

"It's fine. Will the Werewolf Council offer any aid, other than giving out information?"

"No, the Werewolf Council likes to remain passive and seldom get involved."

"What about Victor?" I demand. "Shouldn't they be concerned about a dangerous sacred werewolf running about?"

"They are, so all nearby packs are tasked to kill Victor on the spot. He's too dangerous to live, as he is an unpredictable sacred werewolf that has harmed the more valuable one, Melody."

"You make Melody sound like an object. Besides, I'm destined to kill Victor. I saw it. I'm not sure anyone else can kill him."

Silence settles between us. Using the break in chatter, I move to the bed and get in, lying in the same spot Victor had laid in. I take my sunglasses off and place them on the bedside table. We haven't talked about the elephant in the room. The one important to our relationship.

"Liam, I saw you and Victor kissing," I state emotionlessly, turning my head. I look at Liam, his eyes are downcast. "I can forgive the kiss; you didn't initiate it, and Tegan convinced me it must have been a goodbye kiss. Was it?"

"Of course, it was! I would have told you what happened, I swear on my parents' immortal souls."

"Good to know, nonetheless, like I said, I can forgive the kiss, even though you promised you would not cheat on me." Shame and guilt ebbs into our soul bond. "What I cannot forgive is the relationship with Victor. He is a pureblood extremist. Quite vocal about it too. He was disgusted that Tegan is Beta-Female, just because she's human. That type of prejudice is wrong. And while I agree we cannot trust everything Victor said, somehow in my gut, I have a feeling you two did tell horror stories of hybrids when you were younger?"

"We did," Liam confirms. "Although I stopped it when I was ten because it felt wrong. And I was always uncomfortable when Victor would go on one of his pureblood rants. I did not agree with what he thought. I guess that's why he stopped talking about it." He pauses and his eyes meet mine. "I thought he had become more accepting. I was a fool. Blinded by my feelings. After my parents and brothers died, all I had was JJ and Victor, they were my two true friends. A pack is a huge responsibility and when I took over, a lot thought a fourteen-year-old kid couldn't do a good job. JJ and Victor were the only two who thought otherwise. Within a year, the whole pack started believing in me too." A smile is on his lips, proud of his accomplishment, then falls away, as he continues. "On my seventeenth birthday, Victor kissed me. I wasn't sure if I felt the same way as him, nevertheless, I got into a sexual relationship with him. I did not fuck him here; it was always in his room or in the woods. I'm not really sure it was a romantic relationship; our friendship didn't really change. All that really, altered was I fucked him on occasion. However, when I found out he had cheated on me, I ended whatever was between us. He somewhat proudly admitted to it. Then oddly, he preceded to tell me that he loved me and wanted to be my chosen mate. Nonetheless, I never felt like I wanted to spend my life with him. I think, I'm not sure, I ever saw him other than a friend. I know I must sound like a crappy person. I mean who gets into a sexual relationship with one of their best friends and doesn't see them as anything more than a friend?" Liam wipes away some annoying tears and I find myself, inching closer to him. "The kiss I shared with him today was a goodbye kiss and an apology. For I don't feel the way he does about me. I never did. I told him that after we kissed. That I didn't ever see him as anything more than a friend. No wonder he tried to warn you off, probably wouldn't have even taken much for him to decide to kill you."

I awkwardly pat him on the back, his eyes becoming downcast again. The soul bond continues to be filled with guilt and shame. Sighing, I speak. "I'm happy to know that your relationship wasn't as romantic as I'd imagined. If anything, it sounds like a friends-with-benefits sort of thing."

"Yeah," Liam agrees, "that's how it was for me. Not for him, which makes his cheating a bit of a paradox."

"I don't believe Victor is the sanest person in the world, so don't try to analyse his actions."

"No, I don't think he is. So, are we good?"

"I think so, Alpha-boy."

I encircle my arms around Liam and kiss him. He allows me to be in control, my Alpha-boy allowing himself to be the submissive. I could feel that Liam's story of his relationship with Victor was true, that he did not see it as anything more than friends-with-benefits. Maybe a part of me should feel pity for Victor, I don't. He wasn't fated to be with Liam, I was. Alpha-boy is mine, not his, and no one will get in the way of us.

CHAPTER XII

I rise early. Liam is still asleep, and the sun is just above the trees. Deciding on getting an early start, I put on my sunglasses, brush my teeth, and dress for the day in yesterday's clothing. There is a plethora of obstacles in my life, more than I had on the streets.

The most pressing danger is Victor, for obvious reasons. Then there are the packless attacks, and finally the old threat of my father and his clan. Hopefully, they do not know where I am currently. But they will turn up.

Unfortunately, I suppose Victor may contact my father – the enemy of my enemy is my friend.

Pushing that thought to one side, I leave the log cabin and close the door silently behind me. The early morning is rather humid. I don't expect to see anyone about, but I'm proven wrong by spotting Tegan. She is sitting on the pack house porch, wearing a black long sleeve blouse, tight white jeans and Doc Martens. Trekking over to Tegan, I join her on the porch; Tegan doesn't acknowledge me, her eyes holding a far-away quality.

"Penny for your thoughts?" I ask. "Not that I have any money."

"I wanted that penny," Tegan snarks.

"Sorry, no money here."

"Then I shall not be talking to you."

"What if I asked nicely?" I ask.

"Go on. I'm waiting."

"Please, will you talk to me?"

"Yes, I will."

"Good." I smile happily. "Now tell me what's on your mind. You seem lost."

"I'm not lost, Clay, I'm scared," Tegan begrudgingly admits, her eyes focusing on me. "I couldn't sleep at all last night. I didn't let myself think about what happened until I laid in bed with JJ. I'm not like everyone here, I didn't grow up with the danger of attacks. Nor had I ever felt pain or helplessness like that, yesterday. Victor could easily wipe us out."

"He could and I worry, they might underestimate him because he's just one person."

"You are very bad at comforting."

"Would you rather I lie?"

"No." Tegan sighs, "Can we move onto something happier?"

"Sure, like what?"

"Like, did you punch Alpha Liam in the dick?"

"Unfortunately, not, I decided to go for the civil grown-up way – talking."

"Boo, that's boring. Punching dick is fun."

"I know it is. I punched Victor in the dick."

Tegan grins. "Did he make that sound? That glorious sound that only a man, who's been punched really hard in the dick, can make? FYI, I love that sound."

"He did, but I'm kind of worried about JJ. You don't punch him in the dick for your own pleasure, do you?"

"No, he prefers choking and spanking. My JJ is a freak in the sack."

I laugh, and so does Tegan, the threats that will come momentarily forgotten. There is a kinship between myself and Tegan. One born from being different in a pack of werewolves. Yesterday, as she showed me around the pack house and introduced me to pack members, I could see Tegan knew and was close to many of the individuals she introduced, but there was a divide. Something holding her back from truly being one of them. And there always will be. There is no way for her to be one of them. Werewolves being able to turn humans with a bite is a myth. One that should stay like that. For what if Melody or Victor possessed that ability? Maybe they do. They are allergic to silver and wolfsbane.

If they can, that power could alter the entire world. I need to keep this to myself, until I can ask Melody about this theory of mine. Could the Werewolf Council know about it?

"You look like you need to talk now," Tegan states. "Is it about Victor? You being fated to kill him."

"Maybe," I begin, "I shouldn't have told everyone what happened and what I knew."

"Gossip and secrets spread like wildfire in a pack, remember?"

"I remember," I agree, and I stand. Tegan rises with me. "I'm going to see if Liam is awake."

"I guess I'll see if JJ is awake. See you later," she says, inclining her head, as we go our separate ways.

The trek back is quick, and pushing the door open, I step into the log cabin. My eyes meet Liam's instantly. He sits at his desk in his boxers, and through our soul bond I feel his stress and relief to see me. Leaping to his feet, Liam bolts towards me, entrapping me with his strong manly arms. My stomach churns and I find myself unable to resist my primal need.

Clamping my mouth down onto Liam's throat, my teeth slice into his flesh, his hot angelic blood invading my mouth. Slamming Liam's body against a wall, I kick the door shut and pin his wrists above his head. His hips continuously jerking forwards, matching the rhythm of the moans, escaping his lips.

With a silent command to keep his wrists above his head, I release them so I can explore the unknown lands of Liam's body, starting with his powerful arms, then moving on to his defined pecs and abs. This body is mine, not Victor's, it always was mine, like my body is Liam's.

He's completely helpless to me and in a good way, not the way Victor had rendered him and lots of pack members helpless.

Usurpingly those who worked inside the pack house, did not decide to come outside, even when Victor departed. Though I did see curious kids peeking through the windows.

Unlatching my mouth and straightening, I stare into his half-closed eyes. Drunk on my venom, his lower body grinding against me.

No stress flows through our soul bond, simply lust and hunger. I'm not sure who likes the feeding more, me or Alpha-boy.

"What got you so stressed?" I question, my fingertips tracing the spot on his throat my teeth had torn into. "I doubt my absence caused such a stir."

"Your absence did worry me," Liam shyly confesses, dropping his arms to his side, "but before I decided to look for you, I checked my emails." I glance at his open laptop; I ponder what emails could cause him such stress. "One was sent by Alpha Andrew – the other from Victor."

"Tell me about Victor's first."

"Okay," he agrees. "So, it started with promising I would be his, that nothing would stop him—"

"All very traditional bad guy stuff. What of it?" I interrupted, unimpressed that Victor decided to send a threat through email. "Did he say I was in the way and you would be happier with him?"

"He did. I guess it is very traditional bad guy stuff."

I scoff. "Anything actually important."

His cheeks tinge red. "Victor said he would find the enemy of his enemy and make them his friend."

"So, he will go to my father. Victor is a real cliché with this bad guy stuff. What's next, finding he has double agents among us?"

"Unlikely. JJ and I were the only people close to him. He never was that polite to others. Looking back, Victor hid his rotten nature poorly."

"We rarely see the darkness in those we care about," I reassure Liam. "It doesn't make you a bad Alpha or person."

"Thanks, I really don't deserve you. I don't know how you could touch me as you do – knowing I have been with him."

"You are mine, Alpha-boy, nothing will change that. Now, what about his mother?"

"She's dead. It was a packless attack prior to my parents' and brothers' death. Henri Dupont led it too, so at least I don't need to worry about Victor teaming up with him. He hates Henri as much as I do."

I hum thoughtfully. "Do you think Henri is the one organising, the recent packless attacks?"

"I believe so, but JJ thinks I'm being paranoid and delusional."

"Paranoia kept me alive, and delusions can sometimes turn out to be facts. Now, do tell me, what did Alpha Andrew want?"

"He informed me his son and Melody will be arriving soon. Apparently, Melody had a prophetic dream to do with you."

"Any details given?"

"Just that Melody insisted she come see you, this very instant, and that your life depended on it."

How very dramatic...

CHAPTER XIII

Silently, I observe Liam escorting Melody and Theon into the clearing. Liam left my company five minutes ago, and it has been roughly fifteen minutes since he informed me of Melody's prophetic dream. I remember how Melody said her Sight started with visions and dreams. Has her Sight been restored to its original form?

Jumping off the porch, a childishness I have not felt in years almost urges me to run forward and hug Melody. I manage to refrain; I would not like to embarrass myself.

Melody looks good, all healed and I can smell, no open wounds. Also, at some point, her midnight black hair has been cut, the length an inch or two below her chin. Additionally, colour has returned to her skin and she is dressed, in an oversized men's sweatshirt that reeks of Theon, baggy trousers and mud-stained trainers.

When they reach me, I hand Liam a slice of toast I had taken out of the kitchen; the cooks had already been running about preparing food. He bites into the toast, his eyes focused on Melody.

"We're going to talk alone," Melody states, her dark brown eyes ancient-looking again, though not to the same degree they once were. "Don't either of you dare listen in."

Liam protests as Melody grabs my wrist and drags me around the pack house, past the training ground and into the woods. We stroll in silence for a while and I ponder, where we are heading, until we stop in a meadow full of wild flowers, the meadow Tegan and I talked in yesterday.

"You are well?" Melody asks, her tone of indifference once more in her voice. "Has your time here been pleasant?"

"Yes," I confirm. "Minus the drama with Victor."

"I suppose that has been a bit of a downer. It troubles me that I cannot see him or others like myself. I was idiotic not to realise I had limitations."

"Don't think that, trust me, I'm more idiotic. I didn't even consider the fact I might be immortal." She smiles slightly. "Is your Sight at full strength?"

"No, I'm not. It seems I've reverted." She sighs. "Fortunately, after I woke an hour ago, from my prophetic dream about you, I was fully healed. My wounds gone and my connection to the Sight restored, allowing me to glimpse things in dreams and visions again. Nevertheless, I am not connected to the Sight, in the same way I was when we met. I'm not omniscient anymore." I nod, my heart goes out to her. It must be annoying to have a weaker connection to her Sight. "Are they still arguing?" she asks.

Straining my ears, I hear Theon and Liam verbally fighting. Liam wants to join us, wanting to know what Melody has seen in her dream which could endanger my life. It seems Melody didn't tell anyone what she saw. That doesn't bode well.

"We don't have long," I sigh. "Liam wants to know what you dreamed, while Theon is trying to convince him to wait a few minutes before they come find us."

"Great," Melody says sarcastically, pressing her lips together in a firm line. "First, I will tell you that when I trigger visions now, the future is hazy because of Victor's involvement. Though, I can see that he has or will alter the events of the future, as I'm no longer sure the things I saw will happen. I'm sorry," Melody apologises, "I saw such happiness that might not ever come to be. It fills me with powerful sorrow."

"Do not mourn what could've been."

"I know and I try not to think about the futures that could've been. Unfortunately, everything I have seen is branded into my mind. Although that doesn't matter at the moment, for I must offer you something I did not see when I was all-knowing."

"What is it? Does it have something to do with the dream?"

"Correct," Melody says, and sighs, her dark brown eyes downcast. "The dream showed me three different moments in the future. The first was your death, the second is what I must offer to save you – if you don't, you will die. I've triggered dozens of visions of your near future, to make sure. The only ones where you survive are the ones where you are changed," she pauses, allowing the facts to sink in. "In the third act of my dream, you were different – what happens if you agree to my offer."

My mind flashes to how my future-self looked, his hair cut in a military style, his skin sun-kissed, both his arms had gained muscles and his eyes were human-like, save that my irises were golden and blazed like a thousand-suns at midday. I just know what Melody has to offer will give me the strength to survive and kill Victor. If I don't, I'll die.

Snapping out of my thoughts, I realise Liam and Theon are no longer arguing, they are following our scents. We've run out of time. "What do you have to offer?"

"My sacred blood," Melody states emotionlessly. "It is what I offer you. Do you accept?"

"Yes."

"This will forever change you."

"I know."

I step into her personal space. Melody tilts her head to the side, baring her throat to me. This moment, this choice will affect my entire life. I need to know one thing first. "Why were you drawn to me, Melody? I'm pretty sure there are so many people that needed help. Why was it important to save me?"

"I kept seeing you," Melody reveals, her eyes shining silver. "The people I helped, would encounter you one day, and in the timelines, you weren't around to help them, they were worse off. So, I looked for you using my Sight and saw your past, present and future. In doing so, I discovered a person in need, a person who would die without my help. Parts of your future I saw had a hazy quality to it, a quality that I now know is because Victor is involved intimately in your near future. Yet I could see beyond that haziness. I could see you and Liam in the distant future. Grandchildren running amuck and so very much in love. I knew with my help; you would get that beautiful life and would help those who needed it." Pausing, she catches her breath. "You once asked if I could ever atone. I said no, and that may be true. Nevertheless, by saving you, making your survival possible to help those in need and live happily, I may atone as much as I ever will."

"That's a lot of pressure. You really do have a lot of faith in me."

"I do. You will positively change so many lives. That is a constant in all your futures, Clay. You are a force to be reckoned with."

"One last question – will I live forever? Am I immortal?"

"Yes, that's what makes you a force for good, as you will save countless others if you live."

I swallow deeply. "And the only way for me to live is to accept your offer and drink your blood?"

Melody nods, her neck still bared to me, a vein in her neck protrudes and pulses noticeably to me. Theon and Liam are close, minutes away. I abruptly hug Melody, pressing my face against her throat.

Pushing down, my teeth slice into her flesh. Her blood oozing into my mouth, her blood is thick and acrid tasting. I have to force myself to swallow it. I've never tasted blood like this, and it repulses me. It is an effort to keep it down. Liam's blood has spoiled me. Melody's blood, compared to my Alpha-boy's, is like drinking liquid garbage.

Then, very slowly, the taste of her blood changes, becoming sweet, deadly sweet, too sweet. I'm choking on it, struggling to swallow this thick, too sweet blood. My body is twitching against my will. Melody lowers our bodies, so she is sitting on the ground and I'm straddling her. She is humming. The tune is familiar. I want to release my jaw, so I can purge her blood from my body, but I can't.

My jaw is clamped hard against her throat. Forcing my fangs to stay embedded. Forcing me to continue drinking. Forcing me to further drain Melody. Will I kill her? Did Melody know that I may be unable to stop?

"Maybe this is what I deserve," blood begins to dribble down her chin. *"Maybe, my atonement is death."*

No, I can't be the reason she dies. I can't drain her to death. Please, Goddess, I know I haven't been a true follower. In fact, if I'm being honest, I barely know much about you. However, that is irrelevant, what is important is that you give me strength to stop. I don't want to kill Melody, even though she probably sees this as her atonement.

There is no reply. Once again, Melody's blood changes, no longer sweet or acrid, it is pure pain as if I am drinking lava. My body convulses, my jaw clamps down harder, my teeth baring deeper into her.

I sense Liam and Theon, Melody is yelling, she sounds weak, I can't make out her words.

My eyes scream in agony and my vision abandons me. Leaving me in darkness. My hearing follows quickly after, making my entire universe the blood flowing into my mouth and down into my ravenous stomach.

Alien hands touch me, trying to pry me away. I refuse, my jaw tightening, teeth again baring deeper. Part of me no longer remembers I don't want to kill Melody, all that I know seems to be one thing – I must drink the blood.

The blood's taste changes for a third time. It is sour, making me choke again like her too sweet blood. The foreign hands continue their attempt to pry me away, but all in vain. Nothing will make me release my jaw. Not my gratitude to her, not my morals that have held me back from killing, not even the Goddess can stop me.

Forgive me Melody. Is this what you knew would happen? That I would kill you?

"*Maybe this is what I deserve,*" blood begins to dribble down her chin. "*Maybe, my atonement is death.*"

Had you never stopped believing that? That your only way to atone is that you die? No, Melody, please no. Goddess, please help me, give me the strength, I beg of you! Please!

No reply again. There is no Goddess, maybe magic users and werewolves just evolved from humans. Then they created a deity to explain away how they came to be. It doesn't matter, nothing matters. My first kill will be Melody Morning, the woman who saved me, who has offered her life to me.

"*My sacred blood,*" Melody states emotionlessly. "*It is what I offer you. Do you accept?*"

"*Yes.*"

Why Melody, why didn't you tell me I would take your life? Is it because you knew I would have refused? You deserved to have a happily ever after. Now it is gone forever because of me...

CHAPTER XIV

Pain is the first thing I register. The next is my heart, it beats too slow – inhumanly slow. My eyes open. I'm in an open-spaced room, blood and disinfectant the dominant smell. A curtain is half drawn around the bed I lie on. I can see most of the foreign space, though it doesn't take a genius to guess where. I'm in the Willow pack's clinic.

There are countless hospital beds, their curtains undrawn. A handful of doors lead to other rooms, probably rooms where they do surgery, or rooms with medical equipment.

Listening, I can hear a few voices, one is an unknown female, another is Liam and the last is Theon. They are outside, and Theon sounds furious. Climbing out of the hospital bed, I find my body aches with weakness, making my legs strain to support my body. Stumbling past my half-drawn curtain, I see a hospital bed to my left with its curtain fully drawn around it, and my stomach clenches painfully. A beeping sound resonates behind the curtain – she's alive.

Nervously, I approach, pushing the curtain to one side, revealing Melody's unconscious body. She is again sickly pale, dressed in a hospital gown, and hooked up to several machines. Her throat is bandaged – I did this to her. My eyes burn. I put Melody in a hospital bed. *She's alive,* a voice inside me whispers. *You didn't kill her.*

I would have, I know I would have. I don't remember stopping, I must have passed out. The last thing I remember is thinking how I had ruined her chance of happiness. I'm an abomination. I was actually starting to think I might not be, turns out I'm wrong. Maybe my death would be better for everyone.

I collapse onto a chair positioned next to Melody's hospital bed, shaking with suppressed emotion. I see my face reflected on one of the monitors screens, my eyes blazing gold, the eyes of my future-self. Shock overwhelms me, causing my eyes to change, the pupil thinning into a white slit, my irises turning pitch black while red floods my sclera.

Shivering, I wrap my arms around myself. I notice with surprise, my skin isn't unnaturally white, it has colour, almost sun-kissed. Examining my arms, I realise they are slightly muscular. Frowning, I lift up my tee and see my stomach is toned in a way my scrawny body has never looked. Now, all I have to do to complete how I saw myself in the future is get a haircut.

Though, Melody's sacred blood hasn't just physically changed me. No, it has birthed a new strength and power inside me. What the power I sense inside me does, I'm not sure. My throat constricts as the memory of Melody confirming I'm immortal. Liam, Tegan, Melody, everyone I have ever known will grow old and die around me. I'll forever be alone, like I was for the last two years.

Melody changed that, she altered my life, saved it too. She found me and set me on the path to find a home, to find Liam, to relearn to trust those around me. Well, to a degree, I'm not going to blindly trust people. Although I do trust, I trust Melody, Liam, Tegan and maybe JJ. A short list. But bigger than it ever was during my two years of homelessness.

"I'm sorry," I croak out, my voice trembling. "I owe you so much. Why did you offer your life to me? Did you know you could've died?"

She doesn't reply. Of course, she can't, she's unconscious or worse, in a coma. Anger boils in my stomach, once again my eyes burn, and I know that if I looked at the monitor, my new golden eyes would be boring back into me.

Someone snarls. Glancing in the direction, I see Theon, his Alpha eyes ominously shining. "Get the fuck away from her!"

I stand, surprise filling me, I raise my hands in the sign of surrender. It does nothing to appease Theon, as his nails transform into claws and a thin layer of fur sprouts on his skin. Liam and a female Gamma are close behind Theon, ready to grab him if he decides to attack.

The female Gamma is a tiny, lithe, dark-skinned, brunette woman in her late twenties with warm dark eyes. She is wearing light pink scrubs. She must be a pack doctor. "No one will be attacking anyone in my clinic," she states, her accent vaguely German. "Especially not a patient."

"He did this to her!" Theon growls.

"With permission," Liam argues. "You heard Melody when she shouted at us, she gave permission. It's why she came. And besides, remember your place, Theon. If you attack my mate, I will declare war on Reed pack. And you will have no close allies to help you. Both Miller and Johnson pack would gladly help me wipe you out."

Theon grits his teeth, the fur and claws vanishing, his eyes returning to their human form. However, rage and hatred continue to flow out of him in waves.

My Alpha-boy comes to me, guiding me away and across the clinic. Then forces me onto one of the many hospital beds. I'm not sure it was wise placing my unconscious body in the bed next to Melody's. The emotional Theon could have easily attacked me. Speaking of him, he's drawn the curtain around Melody's bed.

The pack doctor clears her throat, gaining my attention. "My name's Dr Carmen Zeller, I run and manage the clinic. I'm the head pack doctor. You've been unconscious for about two hours; it's just before 9am. You're lucky she lived – you took a lot of her blood. Do you give me permission to run a few tests to make sure you are alright?"

I nod, my stomach somersaulting. I don't feel the burn in my eyes, and I'm looking directly at her. She should be seeing her death. When did the burn fade? It faded when Theon snarled at me. I looked at him and he didn't see his death either. Has Melody's sacred blood purged the magic woven in my eyes, thus severing my connection to the Source?

~

My stupid Alpha-boy fusses, adding more pillows to prop me up and asking me if I want any food. I refuse, the idea of eating makes me nauseous. My body continues to ache with weakness, I wonder if it will ever disappear, or will I have to live with it?

My theory that my eyes no longer give people visions of their deaths is correct. Over twenty individuals have seen my eyes, without adverse effects, which means I don't need any form of eye coverings anymore.

Sadly, if I needed to continue hiding my eyes, I wouldn't have been able to continue using my sunglasses, as the lenses shattered, during my feeding frenzy on Melody.

Dr Zeller ran a lot of tests on me. The single thing that concerned anyone was that my heart was highly irregular, beating very fast, then very slowly. Still, I was released and allowed to stay in the log cabin. Other pack doctors and nurses began to arrive as my tests went underway. Dr Zeller informed me that pack doctors take turns working the night shift, in case someone is injured. However, even if they're injured, it doesn't mean they'll come to the clinic, as werewolves have regenerative abilities, and seldom need a doctor to treat them, unless they are seriously hurt, or have broken bones that need to be properly reset.

A few nurses normally worked alongside the pack doctor during the night shift, but Dr Zeller had let them go off to bed early. She had also been ready to leave early, meaning the clinic would have been closed for at least two hours with no trained professionals, as 9am is when the night shift ends.

If Dr Zeller had left immediately with the nurses, Melody would be dead. Since there would have been no one to treat her. Unfortunately, even with her aid, there is a chance Melody might not wake up, and if she does, she may have permanent damage to her vocal cords. Damage I'll be responsible for.

"Are you really, okay?" Liam asks for the umpteenth time; it is beginning to get on my nerves. "If you are hungry, I can get you anything."

"I'm really fine, Alpha-boy, and I don't need food," I refuse again. "The idea repulses me."

"Do you need blood then?"

I consider the question. The prospect of blood dries my throat and makes me salivate; a clawing sensation emanates in my gut. I'm not repulsed, in fact it makes me hungry and thirsty. It is strange, I have not hungered for blood, I have thirsted for it, yet never hungered.

"I believe," I begin, "that my dietary need is now solely blood-based."

"Then drink," Liam says, offering his wrist.

I've always been a throat guy. Still, I take the wrist and bite down. I'm too parched and ravenous to care where I bite. It is like I had not realised my need until Liam asked.

Alpha-boy's hot angelic blood trickles into my mouth, the flavour is deeper and richer than it once was; Liam moans, his legs shake, trying to support his pleasure riddled body.

The aches and weakness my body has been plagued with since I awoke vanishes. I needed blood to regain my strength. With effort, I release Liam. He stumbles back, leaning heavily against the wall. The scent of his arousal is thick in the air. Blinking a few times, he speaks, his voice serious, and our soul bond becoming full of grief and terror. "When we found you, Melody shouted that she might die, that this was her choice. That for you to survive, you needed to drink her blood. Despite her protests, Theon tried to pull you off. It just made you bite down harder. Then unexpectedly, you went limp and fell backwards. Melody's blood was dripping down your chin, and your sunglasses lenses were shattered beyond repair. Though, you weren't unconscious, no, you were dead," he releases a shuddering breath. "You weren't breathing, and I felt our soul bond dissolve into nothing

– I felt you die. Ten seconds must have passed until you started to breathe again, and with you alive again, our soul bond snapped back into place. Nevertheless, you were dead and you've changed."

"I've changed for the better, and I'm alive now," I state, my heart beating inhumanly fast. I was dead for ten seconds, who wouldn't be freaked out by that fact? "I'm sorry you had to experience that."

"Me too, and I think you should know this. It's something I learned from the Werewolf Council the other day – the blood of a sacred werewolf is lethal to vampires. You shouldn't be alive to tell the tale."

I look down at myself. I should be dead, Melody's blood should have killed me, and it did. My eyes burn. Getting out of bed, Liam tries to help, I wave him off. Standing, I stare at Alpha-boy and for the first time notice that I'm taller than him. His head tilted a fraction upwards to gaze into my eyes.

"Liam, you don't need to worry about me," I miserably tell him. "I'm going to live a long time, I'm immortal. I will be standing when the oceans are no more and humanity is travelling the universe."

"I wondered when I first met you if you were – are you certain you are immortal?"

"Melody confirmed it."

"Then one day, I will be nothing to you. Just a fleeting moment."

I cup his face, my heart wailing. "I will never forget you, and I know we barely know each other, that this is only the third day of us being together. But I can say this with all my heart. I think I'm falling in love with you."

"I've already fallen."

Our lips meet, and the power inside me surges. My arms tremble around Liam's waist. Three days, three years, three decades. It will not be enough. Alpha-boy will never become a fleeting moment to me. Pulling back, I stare into his loving luminous red eyes. "Maybe, I've already fallen too."

His lips stretch into a grin. My heart flatlines, and I glance downwards to see the strange sight of our feet floating off the ground. It seems I can levitate.

A knock sounds and we both drop to the ground, Liam's eyes widening comically. "We were floating?"

I nod and mosey towards the cabin door. Opening the door, my blood transforms to ice. JJ stands beside a woman, a woman who haunts my nightmares and dreams. Her blonde hair is in a French braid, she has vibrant green eyes, muscular arms, arms that could hold a scared little boy. Although, this isn't her, her face is shaped differently, her nose is thinner, and her ears stick out. This is my mother's fraternal twin – Hannah Darby.

CHAPTER XV

It's like I'm underwater. Everything sounds murky. I sit stiffly next to Liam on his side of the desk, with JJ standing behind Aunt Hannah's chair. Aunt Hannah is on the other side of the desk, explaining that she got a call from a friend on the Werewolf Council, that the Alpha of Willow pack in America was looking into her sister. Apparently, there are several packs called Willow pack, except we are the single Willow pack in America.

"So," Aunt Hannah says, in a voice almost identical to Mum's cadence and accent, "why were you looking into Maria? Did you come across a packless that looked like her? Please tell me that's what happened. It's been over eighteen years since I've last saw her."

Liam pats me on the thigh, I know this is him telling me, I can tell the truth or lie. It is my choice.

Licking my bottom lip, I'm not sure what to do. This woman is my aunt, my last living relative that doesn't hate me. Yet that could change in a blink of an eye. She might be a blood purist, blame it all on me. I deserve some of the blame, and I know that, although I did not kill her.

Sighing sadly, I look into her vibrant green eyes and beyond, glimpsing her Delta eyes. Both identical to Mum's human and werewolf eyes. I have to tell her the truth, I cannot lie to those eyes. Pushing down my emotions, the burning in my eyes fade, and Aunt Hannah gasps as my eyes return to their original form. "My name is Clay Knight, I'm the Alpha Male of Willow pack, or have been for three days. Before that in England, I was homeless for two years. And I was homeless because my biological father had found my mum and me," I pause, letting the information sink in. "I'm a hybrid, half-werewolf and half-vampire. I'm not sure if I'm just that anymore, or something new, or what my father believed me to be – an abomination. I'm off track. The day he came, I ran when Mum yelled me to. I lost my home, my mum and my human life on that mundane day." Again, I pause, letting the information sink in. "I had spent sixteen years of mundane bliss, pretending to be a human. So, living on the streets was an adjustment. You might wonder why we weren't in a pack or a clan. The reason being, my father wants me dead. So, we hid among the humans. Mum had no choice. My father, her mate, wanted her to get an abortion. But Mum loved me already and refused, rejecting him to protect me. Then she got a warlock to do a ritual to hide us. And because of that we were safe for over sixteen years. However, the warlock died and the spell that the ritual cast was undone. Sadly, without any warning of his death, we were unprepared when he arrived with his clan. My mum, the woman who died so I could escape went by the name Mary Knight, it wasn't her birth name, it was—"

"Maria Darby," Aunt Hannah interrupts, finishing my sentence. "Your mum is my sister?"

"Yes." Anxiously, I get up and walk over to my bag. I haven't unpacked it yet. Retrieving the photo I have of us, I trudge towards her, handing her my most prized possession. Aunt Hannah's face contorts into one of sadness and joy, in seeing a new photo of her sister.

"She looks happy – was she?"

"Most of the time," I reply. "She got sad sometimes, and when it happened, I could tell. She would smoke excessively."

Aunt Hannah chuckles humourlessly. "I see she didn't drop the habit then."

"No, no she didn't."

"She loved her smokes," she whispers, blinking tears away, before looking at me intently. "Now I know who you are, you do look a lot like your father. Same colour hair and same physique, lean and muscular."

The words are like punches; it must show on my face, as she immediately apologises.

"It's okay, it's just that I'm nothing like him. I'm not a monster, who couldn't love his own flesh and blood. So, do you hate me?"

"Of course not," her eyes shine brilliant orange, both JJ and Liam soundlessly leave, giving us privacy. "You are my nephew. If Maria had told me, I would've gone with you. Nevertheless, she didn't. Though, I guess I wasn't in a good place. My soulmate, Logan, he was human and had recently died in a car crash. We were just beginning to think about children."

"Maybe, Mum thought you would hate her for rejecting my father and getting pregnant," I offer, trying to give an explanation.

"I couldn't hate her, especially when it was to protect her child. My nephew. The last of our family. I never did get to have kids, and we don't have any cousins, so you will be the last Darby."

My heart aches, I would be the last anyway, I'm immortal. "Just so you know, I only found out my true surname two days ago. I should have reclaimed it then, but I didn't. So, I'll do it now." I pause. "My name is Clay Darby, and you are my Aunt Hannah."

Multiple emotions cross her face. She leaps out of her chair, and her body collides with mine. My arms wrap around her at the same time her arms encircle me. She is rather short, and I rest my chin on her head. Shutting my eyes, I inhale her scent, it is so similar to Mum's.

My Aunt is shaking, her silent tears soaking my red tee, as my own silent tears dribble down my face. Mum deserved to have known her sister would have come with her; she deserved to be in this hug with us.

Pulling back, Aunt Hannah stares up at me. "I was wrong earlier; you don't look like him. You look like her. You have the same shape nose and eyes." She frowns. "I didn't like your father; he was always repulsed that my mate was human. I think he was even happy when Logan died. No chance of a half-human and half-werewolf baby."

Something seems off. "What exactly happened, you said it was a car accident?"

"Yeah, it was raining that night, and he must have gone too fast, because the car flipped and he ended up in a ravine. By the time someone found him, he was dead."

"Are you certain it was an accident?"

"Yeah, I'm certain. There were investigations both by police and the pack."

I'm not certain, because I know what type of man my father is. If he's willing to kill his own son because of his impure blood, what would he do to stop a hybrid from being born?

"You said you were thinking about children?"

"Yes, what about it?"

"Did my father know?"

The colour drains from her face as the realisation of what happened hits her. Thomas Blake, my father, her sister's mate, killed her soulmate.

CHAPTER XVI

Liam works away at his desk – we just had lunch. I had a blood bag; I believe I need to feed more regularly.

Aunt Hannah did not join us for lunch. She's resting in a guest room in the pack house, absorbing the information that her soulmate, Logan, was likely killed, by my not so beloved father. Closing the book, I was reading, I return it to one of the bookcases, my mind wandering to Thomas Blake. I've been on the run for two years, and before that I spent years waiting in dread. I want it over; I want my father dead.

I'm tired of having to worry about it, tired of looking over my shoulder, tired of wondering when he will get to me. Father needs to die, and the next time we meet, he will. Should I be worried that I wish to kill him? I haven't killed anyone, save maybe indirectly, like I did with Johnny. Will killing make me a monster? Melody believes herself to be one – for all those she's killed directly and indirectly. Should I really darken my soul by killing him?

I know the answer. Yes, I will kill. I'll kill both him and Victor and anyone who gets in my way. I'm done running. This is my home; I am Alpha Male Clay, and I will protect my pack!

I hear someone approaching the log cabin, so I head to the door and open it. On the other side, ready to knock, is Dr Zeller. She looks exhausted. "I have good news. Melody is awake."

Everything seems to blur. Suddenly Liam is next to me, and we are walking to the clinic. Inside, it is busy. JJ ran combat training today, and there was another attack on the border, resulting in a handful of pack members who need medical care from the two events.

Liam guides me to Melody's bed; the curtains are undrawn. Theon is happily holding her hand and conversing with her. Melody's voice sounds croaky, yet strong. She won't be mute. Though, she will have reminder as she has a faint bite-mark scar.

Theon isn't the only person keeping her company. Ashley is there with Dylan, their Delta eyes glaring hostility at me. Jared is there too; he flicks Dylan's ear, making him exclaim in pain and frown at him. Cathy is next to her cousin, anxiously looking at Theon. Finally, there is a little preteen girl, her red hair in pigtails, blue eyes downcast, dressed in a white long-sleeved dress. She must be Katie, Dylan and Jared's adopted daughter. Dylan protectively moves Katie behind him. Jared once again flicks his ear. This time he doesn't exclaim in pain.

"Clay," Melody rasps, a small smile on her lips. My eyes burn and her smile grows, "it worked, I saved you, changed you." Her eyes close, and Theon frowns. "I can't see much – your future is too hazy now." Melody's eyes open, liquid moonlight bearing into my soul. "I will be of no help. I am blind, nor can I teach you to use the magic inside you. I know someone, a warlock, Nicky, he owes me. He can help."

"The magic inside me?" I enquire. "Is that what I sense? The power?"

"Yes, it is magic that you sense. My sacred blood has strengthened your connection to the Source."

I frown. "Then why don't people see their death in my eyes anymore?"

"Your magic isn't focused solely in your eyes. It flows throughout your body. Shut your eyes and focus inwardly."

I obey, gasping. Goosebumps dance across my skin, and I perceive a peculiar alien sensation in my whole body – I presume this is my magic.

"Papa, Daddy, he's flying!" a childish pubescent voice shouts, and I look down, seeing I'm a few feet in the air, and sparks are popping out of my fingertips.

"Amazing," Liam remarks. "You're amazing, Clay."

Flushing, I slowly lower myself back to the floor, with solely my will.

Dr Zeller steps forward and coughs. "I think Melody should get some rest. Everybody out. Even family."

"Just give me a minute," Melody begs, and Dr Zeller sighs and nods her head. "Theon call the number I gave you, and Jared, will you do what I ask?"

"One haircut coming up," Jared says, then looking at me he asks. "Are you okay with me cutting your hair?"

"Clay doesn't have a choice."

"No, I don't," I agree. "I need a haircut. Can we do it now?"

"That's fine," Jared confirms. Turning to his husband, he says, "Honey, can you head back with Katie alone? I'll go back later with Theon, Cathy and Melody."

"I'll take care of him," Theon reassures Dylan, who looks uncomfortable at the idea of leaving Jared behind.

"He'll be okay," Cathy adds.

Dylan sighs. "If he gets hurt—"

"He won't," Liam states. "At least not in my pack."

"Time's up, everybody out," Dr Zeller orders. "Melody, get some rest before you go home later in the evening."

"Whatever you say, doc," Melody replies, shutting her eyes, as we all exit the clinic. Dylan, Ashley and Katie head to the treeline. Theon loiters outside the clinic, dialling a number on his phone. Cathy stops beside him whilst Jared, Liam and I head to the log cabin, where I will get the haircut, I foresaw in Victor's death vision.

Everything is falling into place. Soon Victor will be dying at my feet. However, his death alone won't appease me. No, my father must die too, and the person organising the packless attacks, be it a stranger or Henri Dupont. Then, myself and Liam will be free, free of danger, and safe to just love each other in peace. No one will stop that from happening.

CHAPTER XVII

Tilting my head, I stroke my jaw. A faint stumble has grown. Teamed with my military style haircut, I see a completely different person in the mirror to the scrawny boy of yesterday. Undressing, I gaze at my naked body. It is peculiar to see what Melody's sacred blood has done. All over, my skin is vaguely sun-kissed. Not to mention that my pecs and stomach are toned. My arms and legs are slightly muscular too, and I've accomplished this without the need to work out. I've gone from a scrawny pale freak to an Adonis. Shaking my head, I pull on my borrowed pyjamas. My new bulk makes the top fit better and allows me to loosen the drawstring of the bottoms. I wouldn't say I could be called cute anymore.

I begin to brush my teeth, letting my mind wander. After the haircut from Jared, who is a professional trained hairdresser, Liam returned to his work and I went back to reading. I had another blood bag at dinner. Aunt Hannah joined us, and we talked about her childhood with Mum.

Aunt Hannah was also there for when we said goodbye to Melody, Cathy, Theon and Jared. They were dropped off outside *Wild Pete's Adventurous Diner* by JJ in one of the vans. Before departing, Melody informed me that the warlock Nicky Parry, who will teach me to use my magic, will arrive at some point tomorrow. She also hugged me and whispered in my ear that I should trust no one. Good advice. I didn't see Tegan again today. JJ told me she's been sleeping, reclaiming the sleep she failed to get last night.

Spitting out my toothpaste, I place my toothbrush next to Liam's and run my hands through my now short hair. Upon exiting the bathroom, the familiar sight of Liam lying on the bed in his boxers meets me. Climbing into bed and under the covers, I snuggle up to him, placing my head on his chest.

"Do you think," I whisper quietly, "that we'll ever get the chance to go on our run?"

"It isn't safe," Liam answers. "It might not be safe for a long time."

"I know that, Alpha-boy, but do you think we will ever get our chance for our run?"

"I hope so."

We plunge into silence as Liam wiggles under the covers, his legs tangling with mine. I don't think we will be able to go on our run until my father, Victor, and maybe Henri Dupont – if he is the person organising the packless attacks – are dead.

It sounds callous, inhuman even, to wish three people dead, and know that I'm fully capable of doing it. That the man, my soulmate, could do it too. I don't need to ask him – I just know if given the chance he would kill them. We are the same in that way.

"Clay," Liam mumbles, "when do you think Victor will return with your father and his clan?"

"Tomorrow or the day after, I think the day after is more likely."

"Do you think we will ever get a mundane day?"

"One day," I say hopefully.

"That day cannot come soon enough."

I chuckle and nod in agreement. I so wish we could have one boring ass day. A day where it is just the two of us. No threats or dangers, just us. Unfortunately, tomorrow won't be a mundane day. As tomorrow, I'm meeting a warlock who will teach me to use my magic.

Lifting my head, I look into my Alpha-boy's stormy grey eyes.

Leaning forward, I peck him on the lips. In a swift movement, Liam yanks me atop of him, then flips our positions, so I'm on my back, and he straddles me, his arse grinding against my groin. At a leisurely pace, he unbuttons my pyjama top and discards it on the floor.

"You're so beautiful underneath me," Liam utters. "This reminds me of our first night."

"I remember," I croak, my body thrumming with yearning.

"Do you know how I knew where you were that night we met?"

"No," I wheeze, my body an inferno of desire. "How did you know?"

"Your scent was lingering on Theon; I doubt anyone else could smell you on him. Yet an Alpha can pick out their soulmate's scent, days after they have been to a place." He smiles proudly, then frowns. "At the prospect of meeting you, I was excited and angry that my parents and brothers would not meet you. Still am. It's why I was a bit cold to you at the start of the conversation in the Range Rover and my introduction to you."

"That explains it, I guess," I say. "Though, even if that's how you were normally, I would love you regardless."

"I love you too and would love you anyway you were," Liam confesses, his face blazing, as his hot lips crash down onto mine. His calloused hands run the length of my naked torso, sending goosebumps all over. He must remember last time well, since his hands eventually halt at my hardening nipples. His skilled fingers tweaking them, rendering me a moaning mess.

I've not truly loved anyone like I have Liam. Once I thought I loved Sabrina. It wasn't love, no, it was merely a schoolboy infatuation. She was embarrassed to be dating me. I could understand why, I was strange. Still, I was heartbroken when she broke up with me.

She had called me over, like we usually did. Like we had been doing for months. Whenever her parents were out, she would ask me to come over. We would have sex, cuddle, and a few times we watched a movie afterwards.

Why am I thinking of her at this moment? Pushing Sabrina to the back of my mind, I refocus on Liam. His tongue slips into my mouth, and his hands are once more exploring the contours of my naked torso.

I don't bother trying to win in a battle of dominance with our tongues. I decide to remain submissive, helpless and in his control. An eternity has passed by the time we withdraw and Liam rolls off me. My body cries at the loss of him. "We should go to sleep; you have a big day tomorrow."

I snort. "When haven't I needed my sleep? Lame excuse."

"I know, I just want our first time together to be special, and I know you agree. You stopped us last time."

"You're right, I want our first time together to be special too."

"And it will."

"Have you made plans?"

"Of course, I have. It will be amazing and romantic," he boasts. "Plus, all our dangers will be put behind us."

"That sounds perfect, though the last one slightly unrealistic," I comment cynically.

"The moment will come."

I roll my eyes. "Goodnight, my Alpha-boy."

"Sweet dreams."

Snuggling up together, I close my eyes. Liam's heart and breathing evens out almost at once. Soon a soft snore is emitting out of his mouth. Three days I've known him, and I love him, I love him so much. I'm scared of what I might do to protect him, to protect this pack, to protect myself. I'm already comfortable and accepted that I will kill my father, Victor, possibly Henri Dupont, and anyone who might get in my way. What lines will I not cross?

Am I an abomination? I don't know, I'm half-werewolf and half-vampire, and I have a connection to the Source, rendering me, basically a magic user, in all but blood. There probably has not been anything like me, or ever will be.

I'm truly special, and other words for being special are freak, strange, monster, abomination, outcast and abnormal. Those words all describe me. I need to accept that. Accept I am different, that there will never be anyone or any hybrid like me.

You are special. Melody said that five days ago, and she is right, I am special, as I am immortal, stronger than any supernatural creature, and possess magic. However, I suppose I always had possessed a bit of magic – the death visions.

Sighing, I halt my thoughts. I need to sleep. Tomorrow, I have magic lessons, and who knows what else will happen.

My days haven't exactly been boring since Melody walked into that café six days ago. I will never be able to repay her. What she's given me are things I did not think I would have again – a home, someone to hold me, and hope for the future...

CHAPTER XVIII

I wake up to the sight of Liam drooling in his sleep. He looks younger and at peace. Rising, I dress in a green tee, jog bottoms and underwear. Then I yank on my combat boots and begin searching for my sunglasses, only to remember they are broken, and I don't need them anymore. The realisation embarrassingly renders me frozen, shocked to my core that I will no longer need to put them on every day. I've worn some form of eye covering every day since I could remember.

My eyes sting with the familiar burning sensation, tears itch, wishing to slide freely down my face. Mum deserves to see me now: happy, free of my cursed eyes and with a man I love. The last time she saw me, I had been sulking.

Biting my lip, I bet a part of her wished I was less of a coward and had stayed to fight. Stayed to keep her alive. Though Melody told me, in the hotel in Lockborough, that I couldn't save her. That I would've died. Still, I wish I had stayed. That I hadn't abandoned her in her time of need.

My mind wonders back to just over three months ago, when Father nearly had me in his grasp. He taunted me, mocked me and insulted Mum, trying to provoke me. I didn't fall for it. I dealt with the daywalkers he had brought easily, snapping their necks like twigs, and escaped.

Snapping a vampire's neck is like knocking a human unconscious. Decapitation and heart removal are the only two ways to kill vampires, that or sunlight if they aren't daywalkers.

Maybe I should have attacked him then, for I did not ever fight him directly. Thinking about it, I guess I did not attempt it, knowing that if I did, I would kill him. I wasn't ready to cross that line then. I am now.

Shutting my eyes, I can clearly picture him in my mind. His chin-length caramel hair that I inherited, vampiric white skin, red eyes full of bloodlust, and a style that looked appropriate in the early twentieth century: three-piece suit, well-maintained Oxfords and a Bowler hat. That was the one thing Mum ever mentioned that she despised. His old-fashioned dress sense.

Mum never knew how old he was. He would not tell her if he was a century or a handful of centuries old, or if he had not been a vampire for long.

Sighing mournfully, I move to Liam's desk and write a short note informing him I'm going on a walk and not to worry. Departing the log cabin, I find myself propelled towards a familiar route to the meadow full of wildflowers. It is like I am drawn there. First Tegan took me there, then Melody, now I'm taking myself there.

The journey is expeditious, thanks to my speed walking.

Upon arrival, I take it all in as if it was the first time. It is a peaceful meadow that contains various coloured wildflowers. I feel a connection here, and as I meander into the middle of the meadow, my magic surges, a few purple sparks springing out of my fingertips.

Someone coughs, and I pivot to see a man and a woman – no, a warlock and a witch.

The warlock is in his early twenties, and has short, curly green hair, a well-trimmed green beard, ebony black skin, and eyes with hot pink irises, horizontal white pupils and violet sclerae. He sports a septum piercing, and his sleeveless tee shows off his bare arms, both with five black tattooed bands. His clothing is finished with distressed jeans and flip-flops.

The witch is younger, about my age. She has a large bushy afro, ebony black skin like the warlock, eyes with orange irises, grey slitted pupils and human white sclerae. She wears a rose red tube top; her navel is pierced, and her arms have the five tattooed bands, identical to the warlock. She also has skin-tight jeans, crocs and hooped earrings.

"You are drawn here too," she remarks, her accent faintly Irish. "He must be the one."

"Yes, his blood sings it," the other replies, his voice has a vague Irish lilt, "can't you hear it, Erin?"

"I do. It is a wee hybrid. His blood sings half-werewolf, half-vampire, and magic thrums throughout his body too."

"Yes, this must be Clay Darby. The one Melody wishes me to teach. Speak, is this true, wee one?" Startled, I bob my head in a nod. "Grand. I'm Nicky Parry, this is my wee sister Erin. We will teach you. First, pray tell, what are you, wee one? Theon just said you had magic. He failed to inform me you were a wee hybrid. So, how do you possess magic?"

I don't know how I feel being called wee hybrid and wee one, though I don't want to argue about it, so I'll just ignore it. I start to explain to them how a ritual was put on Mum and me while I was in the womb, to protect me from my father. I tell them of my encounter with Gretchen, who revealed that magic was woven in my eyes, and explain the death visions. I also mention how I recently gained the ability to see a werewolf's secondary eyes, through their human ones, and vice-versa. Then I speak of Melody's offer of her blood, and the consequences of taking it – of the magic that now flows throughout me.

"Interesting, wee one," Nicky hums thoughtfully. "I agree with the witch's theory. You probably absorbed magic into your eyes while in the womb. Though it is strange, the magical gifts the Source granted you. Do you still see werewolf eyes behind their human eyes?" I nod in confirmation. "That is a rare magical gift among magic users.

Though I've not heard of a magical gift that involved inflicting death visions on others. Do you agree with everything I've said, wee sister?"

"I do," Erin agrees, and she saunters towards me, her smooth hand touching my face, triggering my magic to become a chaotic maelstrom. "His connection is strong. Violently strong. He is an anomaly. I pity the wee one."

Great. She is starting with the nicknames too.

"Indeed, The Grand Coven will brand him a heretic."

"Yes. The Grand Coven will likely desire to kill him. They've feared the day someone who is not a magic user, having a connection to the Source."

My stomach tightens, this is what I need – another threat, save not any ordinary threat, but the fucking magic users' government. Erin drops her hands and strolls back to her brother's side. They seem completely detached, as if they hadn't given me a possible death sentence. I have a feeling Melody and the two of them got on well.

"How do you know Melody?" I enquire.

"She helped me, wee one," Nicky says. "I was captured eight months ago by a deranged group of packless, who used my magic against their enemies. I couldn't harm them, as they had enslaved me with a magical artefact around my neck that made me completely loyal to them."

"He was their weapon for two months," Erin bitterly says. "Our parents, myself and our wee little sister, couldn't find him. We were a mess, and he was in hell."

"I don't blame you, or our parents, or wee Maeve, for being unable to find me."

The two siblings hug, and I can't help thinking that the reason Melody saved Nicky was because he was being used as a weapon. Like she had been by Victor's father. I wonder why Melody didn't tell me that Erin would come with her brother. Possibly she couldn't see it. Her Sight isn't exactly useful nowadays when it comes to my future.

Erin and Nicky separate, their attention returning back to me.

"Can you sense what is here, wee one?" Nicky asks. "Why you were drawn here?"

"I don't know why. I do feel a connection though."

"That's grand, put your hand on the ground and focus," Erin advises. "Then you will understand the connection, wee hybrid."

Sighing, I accept that is who I am to Erin and Nicky – wee hybrid and wee one. Dropping to my knees, I place my hands on the ground and my head implodes. Down below is a network of magic, it spirals off in every direction, spreading across the entire world, and I can see it all. My mind is torn into millions of directions – to the millions of places the magic spreads. This network of magic is the veins of the Earth, pumping life and healing energy into our world.

In places, the magic is weaker, straining to survive where cities have been erected where nature once flourished. It saddens me. I'm sobbing, my magic and body shaking violently. So many places lie in ruin, life struggling to survive, forests being cut down, animals slaughtered, and the waters polluted. The network of magic is floundering, it can't save the world, it is mourning. The network is sentient, begging to save our world, begging us to stop. It begs we do as it desires.

Abruptly, my mind is yanked out of the network as I'm hauled up by Erin and Nicky. Their expressions are not passive, but of awe. I can't support myself, nor can I kill my tears.

"Feck. My apologises, wee hybrid," Erin says. "I didn't suspect you could connect to the ley lines. It is an extremely rare magical gift. Me and my brother sense the nexus-point of the ley lines, located here in the meadow, but we cannot connect as you have."

"It's conscious, you know?" I say emotionally detached. "It begs to save the world. It begs for us to stop. It begs that we do as it desires…"

"Feck. That is not terrifying to hear at all, wee one," Nicky mutters sarcastically.

"Do you think you can stand on your own?" Erin enquires.

"I can try." They let me go, my quivering legs struggling to support me. I continue to hear the ley lines, begging. I also continue to see it spreading into dozens of directions from this meadow.

Wiping my tears, I find myself looking inward, my magic is different. "I'm more powerful."

"Yes, you are, wee hybrid," Nicky concurs, "and I would say you are one of the strongest magic users I've sensed in my twenty-three years."

"I agree," Erin adds. "I haven't sensed anything like it either. You are extraordinary."

"That may be, but what am I?" I ask. "Because I can't be just a hybrid? I'm too different."

"Does it really matter?" Nicky replies. "Is it not enough to be just you?"

I consider the question, is it okay to be just me? Not a hybrid or an abomination – just me. Just wee one.

Last night, hadn't I agreed I would accept being different, being special, being me? So, that's what I'll be. I'll just be myself, and that is enough – for me.

~

We sit on the training ground tarmac in a triangle. I'm the tip, Erin and Nicky the bottom. They decided the nexus-point would be too distracting to teach magic. Little do they know, a few of the ley lines intersect in the clearing. I believe they can't sense or see non-nexus-points, as they have not mentioned the ley lines. For me, the ley lines are within my reach, pulsating. If I wished, I believe I could draw strength and magic from them.

Liam leans against the obstacle course; he looks sleepy, and I can hear the chatter inside the pack house to do with the breakfast rush. When we came here to begin practising, I decided to wake him up and get my morning feed – something both of us love. I also brushed my teeth, as I had forgotten earlier to do that.

Erin is drawing symbols in chalk on the tarmac, while Nicky flips through an ancient tome. The pages are pretty much transparent and written in a peculiar slanting language. What worries me is that my brain understands a lot of the words.

"It's the language of magic, wee one," Erin tells me, obviously noticing my expression and my eyes focused on the tome. "It can take years to completely understand, and to speak those words."

"She utters the truth, wee one, I've had years. And I still struggle to understand," Nicky reveals, shutting the tome and with a snap of his fingers, it vanishes. "We should begin by informing you on the types of magic. There are five main branches: wordless magic, runes, incantation magic, potions and ritual magic."

"Wordless magic is the easiest to master," Erin continues. "You simply think it and it happens." Both her palms explode into flames. "What you've accomplished with magic so far has all been wordless." She begins to levitate off the ground, purple sparks popping out of her ears. "Wordless magic is relatively feeble compared to the other types. It has limits."

Erin lowers herself back to the ground, the purple sparks stopping and the flames in her palms extinguishing into smoke. Nicky has taken Erin's chalk and drawn a few more symbols. Stopping, he hands the chalk back to Erin. "Runes take a certain artistic skill. A single mistake in a rune can have dire consequences." Waving his hand over the chalk drawn symbols, they light up into a myriad of colours. "Now they've been activated, the runes have created a silencing bubble. Can you hear anything other than us, wee one?"

I strain my ears and discover everything is gone, like someone has flicked a switch and plunged us into a different plane of existence. Liam hasn't noticed, his eyes are closed, his face tilted up to the morning sun.

"There are dozens of runes and hundreds of different sequences," Erin states, as if we were talking about something mundane. "The trickiest branch of magic is incantation magic. You have to speak an incantation in the language of magic. It can take decades to become fluent." She raises her arms above her head and cups her hands, mumbling in a peculiar language – the language Gretchen had spoken to open the portal – save this time, I understand some of the words and get the gist of the incantation – *Bring Forth Fire Creature.*

Tendrils of hot white fire are propelled out of Erin's hands. The fire soaring upwards, forming into a flaming creature with the body of a panther, wings like a dragon and a face of a bird.

The tendrils of fire continue out of Erin's hands, connecting her to the creature. It is impressive, as it flaps its monstrous fiery wings and circles the pack house, its beak opening to release a stream of blue fire.

"That's enough, wee sister," Nicky grunts, and Erin balls her hands, extinguishing the tendrils of flames, and without the tendrils, the creature dissolves into nothing. "I think Clay understands the strength and risk that incantation magic can pose."

I flush. It is strange him calling me by my first name. It seems I have gotten used to my nickname.

"So," I state, "don't attempt it if you don't know the words you're speaking?"

"Correct. We shall teach you a few incantations to help you, wee one. Moving on, potions is the one form of magic we will not be teaching you, for two good reasons—"

"We are shite," Erin interjects, "and we don't have the ingredients or caldron to teach you."

"My wee sister speaks the truth, we don't have equipment or ingredients, and we aren't talented when it comes to brewing potions. My green hair," Nicky gestures to his face, "is a side effect of a potion blowing up in my face, literally. I'm sorry to fail you in this. Someone with your power deserves to know and perform all the basics. Maybe if Maeve was here, she could teach you. She's an adequate brewer. However, at the moment she is travelling with our parents."

"That's all right, no need to apologise," I say. "Potions aren't going to be useful to me at the moment. So, what's ritual magic like?"

"Ritual magic is what was placed on you," Nicky states. "Ritual magic is purely protective and restorative. You can heal a minor injury wordlessly, but to heal someone fatally ill or fatally injured, you need to perform a ritual. Ritual magic involves a blood sacrifice, with the incantation of *I offer my blood* or *I offer this sacrifice*."

Goosebumps jump up my spine. He spoke the two incantations in the language of magic, and I understood perfectly.

"The ritual magic placed on you was probably the ritual of secrecy. It renders those who are infused invisible, intangible and untraceable to the supernatural."

"Ritual magic is also used to give back to mother-nature, the Source and the Goddess, if you are religious," Erin states, lowering her arms to her side. "Our family, we do several rituals a year, thanking the Goddess, the Source and mother-nature. It is usually more potent when performed at a nexus-point."

"And that's it."

"No, it's not. There are subcategories of magic," Erin argues, disagreeing with her brother, whom had proclaimed *that's it*. "Like necromancy and divination. Clay's death visions I believe would fall under the latter and former."

"Subcategories of magic don't count, wee sister. Necromancy is an off-shoot of incantation magic and ritual magic, while divination is a combination of runes, wordless magic and a natural magical talent."

"Magical gifts or magical talents are innate abilities," Erin elaborates. "Like your magical gift to see werewolf eyes behind human ones," Erin pauses. "My brother, my wee sister and me have a different magical talent – we can talk to animals."

I laugh. "You got to be kidding me?"

"Sadly not," Nicky groans. "You have no idea of the fucked-up stuff animals discuss. They're either psychotic, depressed or manipulative cunning beasts."

"Some are a tiny bit tolerable," Erin mumbles, her eyes flicking downwards. "I'm going to disable the runes." Her hand glides over the runes, causing them to fade into oblivion. Runes must have a one-time use. The world outside the bubble greets my ears. "What should we do first?"

"We should see what the wee one is capable of, with his wordless magic first."

"Agreed."

They stand in unison. I, on the other hand, awkwardly scramble to my feet in shame. Liam's eyes have opened, I suddenly feel seriously under pressure. Glancing behind me, I see Tegan, JJ, Aunt Hannah and a few dozen pack members gawking at me. Waiting to demonstrate my magical prowess.

Shakily, I raise my hands and imagine them bursting into flames. My magic obeys, and I imagine the fire extinguishing. My magic obeys again. I will myself to levitate, and I do, floating untethered, fifteen feet into the air before forcing myself back down. Next, I telekinetically lift Erin and Nicky, knowing if I wished I could throw them high into the air, then hard back down, breaking every bone in the body – I don't, they haven't wronged me.

I attempt three more magical feats, healing a small cut I inflicted on Tegan. JJ growled at me because I hurt her, then I tried telekinetically pushing someone. Liam was the unlucky participant, he landed on his back, hard. Finally, I blasted a bolt of electricity out of my fingertips, which briefly set part of the obstacle course on fire.

By that point, I can feel my magic has been partly depleted, and I almost desire to feed again on Liam, who I think is slightly pissed off at me. I mean, I did telekinetically push him. I probably would be mad if he did that to me.

"You have a good control of wordless magic," Nicky says. "The rest shall be rather boring."

"Yes, it will," Erin echoes. "And hard work, let us crack on, wee one."

CHAPTER XIX

My magic is completely depleted, and Liam had to carry me, bridal style, from the training ground to bed. Currently, he's at his desk working, and JJ is instructing combat training again. Late, because I used the training grounds for my magical training. Sucking the last drop of delicious blood out of my blood bag, I glance at Liam; he is working through our lunch.

Erin and Nicky have given me at least ten books to study. Books they conjured out of nothing. One of them is just a translation book for the language of magic. Others explain rituals and how to perform them. One is how to make potions, and several are pages crammed with incantations. Another is how to draw runes and the sequences you can put them into. I'm not sure I will see them again. They taught me the basics and now have left to visit Melody.

The blood I drank has returned some strength and magic to me. Though my magic is like a puddle, slowly growing back towards its original maelstrom size, which rages throughout my body. Climbing out of bed, I stumble towards Liam, collapsing into the chair next to him. He side-eyes me, he's still mad that I telekinetically pushed him.

"I'm sorry," I tell him. "I didn't mean to hit you that hard."

"It was embarrassing."

"Do you want to push me then?"

"Of course not!" Liam exclaims. "I would never purposely harm you to get even."

"Then you are a better man than me, Alpha-boy."

He chuckles and I rest my head on his shoulder, listening to his heart and the typing on his laptop. My mind drifts to my magic. I've mastered and memorised a few simple incantations. I can draw several rune sequences. I know of, and might be able to perform, a few rituals. My wordless magic might need further exploration, and potions – I'll start studying later. Nicky recommended once I recovered that I might spar against someone, so I can get used to using my physical abilities and magic in tandem.

"I think I'm going to go on a walk," I mumble.

"You shouldn't. You've had maybe fifteen minutes rest."

I sigh. "I know, I'm just bored."

"Of course," Liam snorts. "You were literally learning how to do magic. And now you have to rest. I would be bored too. Nevertheless, you need to rest because you didn't even have enough energy to walk back here."

"Okay, I get it, idiotic idea."

"I'm sorry," Liam apologises. "I didn't mean to come down on you so hard." His fingers are a blur of movement on his laptop keypad. "I would like to entertain you, but I need to try and close this deal. Could you attempt sleeping?"

I nod. "I'll leave you be."

Forcing myself out of the chair, I giggle inwardly. How could I think I had enough energy to go on a walk? I can barely stumble back to bed. Tugging the furs and blankets around me, sleep weighs at my eyelids. It appears I don't need to work at sleeping.

However, before I can fully emerge myself into the comfortable embrace of oblivion, something tugs on my consciousness, an invisible string of sorts.

I'm incapable of resisting, and I'm pulled – out of my body. Looking down, I see my own sleeping body from above, while Liam continues to type away on his laptop.

My body is transparent, am I a ghost? I make an effort to scream, yet no sound escapes my mouth. The invisible string tightens, the sensation originating in my solar plexus. Violently, I'm yanked through the ceiling, my body intangible, but no discomfort arises, it is like moving through water.

I'm past the roof. The invisible string goes taut, and I'm flying away at an unnatural speed. Everything becomes a haze of green, then unexpectedly, I halt, hovering above a pile of dead pine cones.

Blinking I spot someone, cowering under the root of a great oak, someone I did not think to see again – Gretchen.

She wears a blood splattered pink-polka-dot dress, and no footwear. Her hands push a wool cardigan against her bleeding gut. Primal terror fills her feline eyes, and clumps of her grey hair litter the ground. She is mumbling in the language of magic, apologising to me. She has somehow accidentally brought my soul to her, as she is not mentally aware enough to intentionally do so. Or in more magical wording, she caused me to astral project to her. I suppose this is an example why one doesn't speak an incantation they don't understand.

Then, like a switch has been flipped, my ears are overwhelmed with the sound of screams, gunfire, fire crackling and fighting. Pivoting towards the source behind me, my eyes focus on the smoke rising above the treetops. The screams seem to reach a horrifying crescendo.

"This is my fault," Gretchen whimpers in English. I spin back to look at her. "If I hadn't helped, this would have been delayed. Forgive me, Clay Darby, son of Thomas Blake and Maria Darby, forgive me." Her eyes lock with mine, maybe she did bring me here on purpose. "Your father is coming for you. They all are. And they've made sure you won't have allies. Johnson pack and Miller pack are under attack, just like Reed pack is."

My stomach drops, and my voice somehow escapes my lips. "What have you done?"

"All I did was open the portals. Victor was the one to unite them – their goals align," she says with a sob. "Thomas wants you dead,

Henri wants Willow pack destroyed, and Victor wants your soulmate. I didn't realise everything until it was too late."

"What did you think was happening?" I snap.

"I thought we were going to kill you. You shouldn't exist, especially the strength of the magic you possess."

Chills go down my spine. "How do you know about that?"

"They have a spy – it was my idea to send them. Can you forgive me Clay? I did not know they were going to wipe out these packs! Please, forgive me."

I frown. "Why do you need my forgiveness?"

"Because my desire to see you, a half-breed, dead, has sped up the genocide of innocent purebloods. I need you to forgive me, or the Goddess will not welcome me into the afterlife, and I will forever roam this world invisible to all. Forgive me. Please..." She trails off, her eyes focused on something else, I turn again. Seeing a man woven out of my nightmares.

"Father," I breathe out, that one terrible word, and it sucks all the bravado out of me. How could I believe I had the strength to kill him?

Seeing him again in the flesh returns me to the first time I saw him – the day I lost everything. He wears an immaculate black three-piece suit and bowler hat; his chin-length caramel hair sits perfectly in place. Absentmindedly, he wipes blood from his mouth, using a handkerchief. All the while his crimson eyes glare through me to Gretchen.

"Please, don't. Please. I can still be useful," Gretchen begs, her pleas now addressed to my sperm donor. "I'll do anything. Please, Thomas." He strolls past me. "Haven't I helped you well? I opened the portals that brought you and your clan here to America, upon getting word the abomination might be here. And I was the one who said you shouldn't attack Henri and his group of packless. That they could be useful. Wasn't I right?" Gretchen is rambling, convulsing in utter terror as Thomas kneels next to her. "Then Victor arrived and united the two of you. If you had killed Henri and his group of packless, this achievement would have been impossible. Haven't I earned the right to live?"

"No." Father smiles comfortingly, one of his hands patting her on the cheek. "You haven't. You're spineless and I don't trust you."

"You can. I'll stay with you. I'll be good. You can trust me."

"My sweet young girl," Father tells Gretchen, her elderly face a stark contrast to his youthful, thirty-something face. "You just lied to me."

And with a fast, easy movement, Gretchen's head is torn off her body, a torrent of blood gushing from her headless corpse.

CHAPTER XX

Eyes flying open, I roll out of bed, landing in a crouch. Liam rushes to my side, eyes-wide, and assaults me with questions. There is no time to talk. I grab his wrist. Following my instincts, my magic penetrates his mind, filling it with what I had just witnessed and learnt.

"Go," I command, "you need to move!"

Liam doesn't respond. He's frozen from the horrors and knowledge I've shown him.

I shouldn't have gone towards the battlefield. I should have returned to my body straight away. Instead, I went to the clearing where Reed's pack house and clinic was. However, both were no more. Simply flaming structures littered with blackened corpses.

Vampires and fully-shifted packless ended lives left and right, as easily as breathing. Other innocents were shot to death from a safe distance. There was no discrimination in who died. *Stop!* a voice inside my head shouts. *No more thinking, it is time for action, playtime is over.*

Standing, I shove Liam, he stumbles backwards. Blinking, Alpha-boy nods and we bolt to the door. I fling it open, and he runs outside, ahead of me, releasing a deafening howl. My depleted magic swirls inside me, a raging storm, and multicoloured sparks explode out of my fingertips. JJ and pack warriors rally to Liam's side, their combat training forgotten as he shouts orders.

Soon pack warriors, who must have been on border patrol, emerge from the treeline, followed by injured and frightened individuals: refugees. Dr Zeller and many other pack-doctors rush to guide the injured refugees into the clinic. Tegan and Aunt Hannah also help in this endeavour. I don't know what to do, there is so much I could do – what should I do?

The Goddess answers my question. Erin materialises out of thin air with Dylan, Jared and Katie. Dylan is the only one standing. He cradles Jared in one arm, Katie in the other. Jared is unconscious, his left arm bending unnaturally, and Katie is sobbing. Tegan begins guiding them to the clinic.

I dash towards them; Erin looks at me relieved. "We need to put up a force field to protect us, wee one. Repeat the words after me." She switches to the language of magic, and I understand every word as if it was English. "*Protect us. Protect this land. Protect us from those who wish us harm.*"

I repeat after her, causing the small slither of magic inside me to disappear into the spell. The sky darkens as black ominous clouds roll into being, swirling downwards and blocking out anything outside the clearing, plunging everything into darkness. A few seconds pass until the ominous black clouds became opaque, returning light to the clearing.

We stop chanting and collapse to the ground in unison, our bodies and magic exhausted. We've done it. I see pack members pass through the force field, sending ripples through the opaque dome structure. It will keep us safe in the clearing. Erin struggles to her feet and wobbles towards my mate, probably to explain what we did.

Aunt Hannah appears next to me, lifting me to my feet. "Are you okay, Clay?"

I nod and lean heavily on her; magic depletion is horrible. I wonder where Nicky is. Once again, the Goddess answers my question as Nicky materialises a few feet away, and in his arms is a baby. Nicky appears to be in shock and hurt. Someone has raked their claws across his left eye leaving five deep diagonal cuts, so deep, I have no doubt his eye is gone.

Nicky's remaining eye is downcast, staring at the crying baby, droplets of his blood splashing down onto the babe. A pack doctor takes him by the shoulder and starts leading him to the clinic. It seems Dr Zeller and her co-workers will be busy like never before.

"Let's get you to lie down," Aunt Hannah says, ushering me into the log cabin, and locking the door behind her. "Come on, get in bed young man. You need to rest. All the magic you've done must be strenuous on you."

"It is." I can't muster the energy to stand on my own. "Help me."

"Of course, nevertheless, we should get you out of those dirty clothes." She smiles kindly, helping me remove my combat boots, jog bottoms and tee, before guiding me onto the bed. "Isn't it terrible what is happening?"

"Yes, it is." My eyes are too heavy to keep open. "They're committing genocide."

"And there is someone to blame, isn't there?"

"Victor."

"No, darling – you are to blame."

Pure agony erupts inside me. My eyes rip open to see my aunt, her hand plunged inside my chest. Her other hand wraps around my throat, choking me. Hatred shines in her Delta eyes. "I'm a good actress, aren't I, nephew?" She spoke the last word like an insult. "My sister should have killed you a long time ago. Your impure blood is a disgrace to the Darby name."

"Logan?" I choke out the name.

"His accident wasn't your father's fault, if that's what you're asking. It was a misdirection. I caused his death. I jumped onto the road in wolf form. He swerved to avoid me. The car flipped and he broke his neck in the process. I was disgusted to be soul bonded to a mere human. Everyone in the Goldstein pack knew it wasn't an accident. It's why Maria hid herself and you." She chuckles humorously. "It wasn't just because of Thomas. For I believe, my sister suspected, I would have ripped you out of her stomach – like

Thomas should have. That was his mistake." My eyes water, her hand inside my chest cavity, wraps around my palpitating heart. "You are very stupid nephew, so trusting, you welcomed me with open arms." Because you look like her, I want to shout. Yet I can't, the grip on my throat is too tight. "Thomas wanted to be the one to kill you – he won't be – I will. All it takes is one good yank."

She laughs, a cruel victorious smile spreading across her face – a smile Mum would never have had on her perfect, beautiful face. Hannah is a disgrace to her memory.

Mentally, I stretch my consciousness outwards and locate the ley lines that intersect in the clearing, their magic and strength surging into me.

Mum always spoke about Hannah in a bitter way. I mistook it, and her seldom talking of her sister, as longing, when it was concealed hate. *Do it, my sweet boy, kill her,* Mum's voice echoes in my mind. *She's another reason I had to hide us. A reason we had to pretend to be normal. A reason your eyes weren't normal. Kill her, my sweet boy. Do it!*

"Any last words," the bitch, formerly known as Aunt Hannah, enquires savagely. The grip on my throat loosens, allowing me the pleasure to speak. "Because I want to remember this moment, your powerlessness. Believe it or not, I was actually impressed by you. I chased after you, you know. But you were always hard to track and a master at losing tails."

Memories of paranoia about being followed surface in my mind. *Paranoia kept me alive, and delusions can sometimes turn out to be facts.* I guess what I told Liam was true. My paranoia kept me safe from getting sneak-attacked, by an unknown danger.

Then if that's true, why didn't Melody warn me? No, she did warn me. Melody told me to trust no one before she left last evening. Nevertheless, that begs the question, why didn't she tell me outright that the bitch wanted me dead? I gasp, my thoughts forgotten, that bitch just dug one of her nails into my heart.

No more thinking. Playtime is over. This is real life and death.

Mum would want me to kill this living plagiarism of her, and I shall. All the magic I have drawn from the ley lines, I now direct at her, its raw power invading her body.

She screams, her hand releasing my bruised and angry heart. She convulses, her invading appendage flying out of my chest. Using a small fraction of the ley lines' magic, the gaping hole in my chest knits back together.

Sitting up, I gaze coldly upon my first intentional victim. Her skin greys and dissolves into ash, foam dripping out of her mouth. Her eyes liquify, blood oozing from her ears, and brain matter creeping out of her nose.

"Mercy," the bitch chokes out, through the foam in her mouth. "Please."

I laugh. "There is no mercy," and I observe distantly as she is transformed, even the liquids escaping her body, into an ordinary-looking pile of ash. "This is what you deserved."

CHAPTER XXI

The bed is cold. I don't think Liam slept with me last night. I can sense my magic is at full power, a raging storm ready to be used. Sitting up, I glance at the bathroom. Hannah's ashes got the burial she deserved – down the toilet. She was a spy, a blood purist, and probably complicit in the planned genocide. I dutifully enlightened Liam and then went to bed.

When I informed him, I went outside in my underwear. I couldn't be bothered to put clothes on. He was busy ordering his pack warriors about. A handful of them were being sent out to look for survivors. If I had more energy, I would've gone looking too, I couldn't. The ley lines, magic and strength were the two things keeping me running. The moment I disconnected, I knew I would be out of commission, and I was.

So, I revealed to him that the bitch was a spy. That she tried to kill me. And that I flushed her down the toilet. I'm not a hundred percent sure everything I was saying got across. It was the first time he had seen me in that state of undress. Once accomplishing that duty, I headed to bed and fell into oblivion.

. . .

Lugging myself out of bed, I sluggishly pull on a yellow tee, jog bottoms, my combat boots and a dark navy hoodie, that I steal out of Liam's closet. Quickly brushing my teeth, I then stomp to the door, thrust it open and stroll outside.

The force field is still running, ripples quivering across the magical domed structure. It is early morning. Overnight, and probably during the afternoon, medium sized metal fences have been constructed across the clearing permitter, a second line of defence against intruders, though easily enough to climb over on either side.

Pack warriors patrol alongside the metal fence. Everyone continues to be on high alert. There are also a few pack warriors, guarding the clinic and the entrance to the pack house.

Not far from the entrance is Tegan sitting on the porch, a cup of coffee in her hands, dressed in a navy sweater, jeans, knee-length boots, with guns strapped on either side of her waist. I walk over to her and plop down. She takes a deep swig of her coffee. Taking a sniff, I realise it has alcohol in it.

"I don't think I'm made for this life," Tegan sighs regretfully. "I love JJ with all my heart, and the three years I've been with him are the best of my twenty-one years. But everything that is happening is a bit much," she sighs again. "It's going to be his twenty-second birthday in two days, and I doubt we will be celebrating. I know I sound horribly selfish. I've heard what's happened, seen the survivors. At one point, I was practically treating patients because there were so many. I'm just not sure I can continue doing this."

"Do you want to leave?" I deadpan.

"JJ wouldn't come if I asked. His place is at Liam's side. He would not desert, not in a million years."

"Loyalty like that is hard to find. And if you left, I would lose a good friend."

Her eyes meet mine; silent tears flow down her face. "You would lose a great friend indeed. I swear this emotion stuff isn't normally me. Why am I acting like such a damsel? This is your second time comforting me, when our relationship started with me comforting you. How times have changed."

"The student becomes the master."

"You will never be the master."

"No, I won't, and you shouldn't be scared. They should be scared of you. You are a strong gun-shooting woman, deserving of the title of Beta-Female," I take the cup of coffee from her and empty it onto the ground. "Now go, spread your wisdom and help those who need it."

"I'll try. The refugees who have been medically cleared have been set up in the spare bedrooms. I'll see if they need anything. I just wish I wasn't merely human. Then I could do much more," Tegan confesses, and with that, she takes the empty cup, stands and meanders into the pack house. The pack warriors guarding the entrance have remained silent pillars. I hope this is one secret that won't spread like wildfire.

Everyone is scared, and Tegan has more reason to fear than many. She is at a disadvantage.

If Melody is in the clinic, I can ask her about my theory that sacred wolves might be able to turn humans into werewolves.

However, the moment I stand, my eyes land on Liam. He is trudging by, his stormy grey eyes half-lidded and his mouth pressed into a firm line. I have to fight every instinct inside myself, not to run to him and yell that he must rest. Except, I can't – this is a time of war. A time where an attack could come at any moment. Everything I ever faced was simply child's play, but playtime is over, the game begins, and there is no more running or hiding. There is just the winner and the dead.

Behind Liam is an equally tired-looking JJ, who uses his metal staff like a crutch. Liam mumbles something about contacting the Werewolf Council again, and JJ grunts in response, the two of them trudging to the log cabin. Shaking my head, I discard my plans of asking Melody. It might have been an impossible task; she could be dead.

I trek around the pack house, a nagging urge to release some frustration. That urge is speedily repressed upon seeing Erin sitting in the centre of the training ground, cradling a baby. A baby swaddled in a furred blanket.

She doesn't offer any greeting or acknowledgement as I sit next to her. She is solely focused on the baby.

Erin has a fleece jacket on, the warmth of the past days forgotten, an unsettling frigid temperature has taken its place. I wouldn't be surprised if it started to snow.

Observing the baby, I notice it has heterochromatic eyes. The right a piercing blue, the other a dull brown. Looking past the unique human eyes, I perceive silver. The baby is a sacred werewolf. It can't be that old, maybe a few months?

"You can sense wee Cordelia is special, wee one" Erin says, her voice in awe. "Nicky was drawn to her, felt compelled to save her. Except her blood sings she is an ordinary werewolf."

"No, she's a sacred werewolf."

"That explains it. Magic users can't detect sacred werewolves like Melody – or this Victor."

"How can magic users detect what someone is?" I ask, a question that has been bugging me. "And what does 'her blood sings' mean?"

"It is called identity magic; it is a form of magic we use to hear ones' blood song. Identify magic is a subcategory of wordless magic and divination." Erin licks her bottom lip. "Most magic users master identity magic by adolescence. You just listen and the blood songs flow into your ears. Give it a go."

I nod and attempt to listen. My hearing can make out hundreds of conversations, exclamations of pain and snoring. I can also hear animals in the forests and the distant screams of agony, as people's lives are put to an end. Then abruptly, like my ears have tuned in to the correct frequency, I hear it. The blood songs, and every species has a different tune. The melodies all merge together – werewolf, magic user, human – I can even hear the blood songs that belong to vampires too, though they are distant.

Straining, I make out my own. The blood songs of werewolf and vampire clash inside me, although under the clashing songs of my impure blood is my magic, constrained and wishing to break free.

Under Erin's blood song, I know her own magic is doing the same. Magic is not meant to be contained indefinitely; it is meant to be used.

Taking a deep breath, I start to tune out the blood songs, until it is a barely noticeable noise in the back of my mind. "My blood's song is agony; it should not be heard."

"I think there is a charm in it."

"I disagree. Yet, I think we should discuss more serious things now."

"Indeed. A war is coming, wee one. Hundreds have already paid the price. Last I heard, only ninety-eight refugees have survived the genocides of Reed, Miller and Johnson pack. My brother wishes us to bail, to prove everyone right in what they believe of magic users – that we look out, simply for ourselves. Except that won't be happening, I will not be fleeing." Electricity crackles and sparks in her afro. "Not after what I saw those bastards do. Innocents killed without remorse. Some took joy out of it. I will never forget it, wee one."

"They will be coming soon," I state tensely. "I could hear the blood songs of vampires in the distance."

"That is good, better they come, wee one. Though, they need to come soon, as with the number of pack members and refugees, food supplies will last a few days maximum."

"Then we must, if it comes to it, be prepared to hunt. Better that than starving."

Our conversation is interrupted, as Cordelia bursts into tears, and Erin futilely tries to comfort her.

Something inside me urges to hold her, so I take Cordelia. All she needs is to be rocked thrice, and she stops her tears. Opening her eyes, she reveals they are now the colour of liquid moonlight.

"Does Cordelia have parents?" I enquire, already sensing the answer.

"No, Nicky found the mother dead, she was still holding her. I asked among the refugees, and it was Theon—"

"Theon is alive?"

"Yes, and it's rude to interrupt. Melody is also alive, although she did not survive unscathed. Additionally, before I spoke to Theon, Melody told me her mother and Theon's father died in the attack." My heart falters, Ashley was a good woman, and Alpha Andrew gave me his pack protection. They didn't deserve to die. I can't help wondering if they ever acted on their feelings for one another? "As I was saying, Theon told me Cordelia's name, and that he saw her father die, making Cordelia an orphan."

My heart twists painfully as I look down at Cordelia's innocent, liquid moonlight eyes. Fury blossoms inside me. She will grow up without parents because of Victor. Handing her back to Erin, I stand, knowing what I plan to do is stupid and selfish.

"Be careful," Erin mumbles, guessing my plan.

I will kill Victor. He united my father and Henri Dupont. Victor is the catalyst that made the genocides possible. He will be the first to pay, and he won't see it coming. For who would expect the prey to become the predator?

CHAPTER XXII

My whole life, I've been the prey – running, hiding and reacting. I've not been the predator. I've never been the one to act first. I've never been anything but a coward. If I had killed my father in the past, the genocides would not have happened. And if I had killed Victor, when he was shocked upon seeing his death, he would have not united them.

Sneaking out of the clearing was easy, too easy. All it took was some wordless magic that rendered me invisible – an invisibility I've kept, as I silently hike through the woods. No sticks or leaves crunch under my feet. How times have changed. I've come prepared, and I have the weapon that will end Victor's life – a butcher's knife, the blade transmuted to silver with a simple incantation. It is grasped tightly in my right palm, the silver blade refracting the morning sunlight.

Crouching, I stare at what is in front of me, roughly fifty feet away – a camp. Packless and vampires mingle, the canopy of trees casting a safe darkness for non-daywalkers. Hundreds of tents are erected, a mixture of smells billowing from the site. Straining my ears, I locate Victor. From the sound of his voice, I would say he is in the centre, talking with my father and an unknown Frenchman – Henri Dupont.

The three are discussing attack strategies, how to bring down the force field, and their numbers. They believe they have roughly three hundred packless and just over a hundred vampires – Henri mentions they have only lost fifteen packless and three vampires.

I grind my teeth. They have only lost eighteen individuals – while hundreds of ours died, literally hundreds. Pushing my anger down, I continue to listen. Victor complains about my father killing Gretchen, and how she could have been used to demolish the force field. My father doesn't take the comment well, and calls Victor a bedwetting child.

The two argue passionately, until Henri ends it, stating they won't have to put up with each other much longer. The meeting ends.

Father is heading to Lockborough, so that he can turn more humans. Henri will see if he can rally more packless, and Victor will make sure no stragglers make it to Willow pack.

That decision will leave him relatively alone. Three vampires and two packless Deltas will accompany Victor. I will kill them too; they have blood on their hands, and I've already killed one person on purpose.

The small group hikes out of the safety their camp provided, stupid prey. I follow Victor and his allies at a distance, none of them aware of the looming threat.

I've not been the stalker, nor the first to strike. It is strange.

The packless Deltas stick close to Victor, the three vampires aren't as smart. They're easily ended, no sound escaping their mouths. One second, they were the living undead, next they are corpses on the ground. Their useless un-beating hearts discarded next to them.

That's how you do it, bitch, I sneer mentally, *one hand in, grasp the organ and yank out. No gloating, no taunting, just do it.* Briefly, I pause, overcome with shock at my callousness. I killed the bitch yesterday, it was her or me, I chose myself. This is different. I killed three vampires who couldn't understand what was happening to them. One second, they were walking, sticking to the shadows, since they weren't daywalkers. Next thing they knew, something was ripping their heart out.

Have I become a monster like Melody believes herself? No, this is different, I'm different. I'm killing not for myself, I'm killing to protect, to avenge our dead, to save lives. I will not regret this.

I continue my stalking. Victor and the packless Deltas unaware of their missing members.

Is this what my father felt anytime I was almost in his grasp – hungry? Not for blood, food, or sex, but the sweet release of taking the life of the deserving. I feel myself salivating at the idea of their dead bodies. One of the packless Deltas, a woman in her early thirties, halts, telling Victor and the other packless Delta to continue without her. She needs to pee. They agree, too idiotic to realise they're being hunted.

Once Victor and the other packless Delta are out of sight, I creep behind the squatting woman. Her trousers and underwear at her ankles. Unaware that death approaches, and like my father did to Gretchen, I pluck her head off her body. A geyser of blood spurting from her headless corpse, drenching me.

Dropping her head and my invisibility, I run, chasing the scent of Victor and his last protector.

Arriving in a tiny field, I see they've found a survivor – a plump boy, no older than nine. He weeps, begs and screams, convulsing under Victor's pain infliction gift. The Goddess should not have blessed him.

The packless Delta laughs and mocks the little boy. His taunts and laughter die though as I snap his neck, his body hitting the ground lifeless. The little boy's screams stop, his eyes transfixed onto me – a creature of death. Victor pivots to stare upon me. Before he can do anything, my magic surges out, freezing him to the spot, and his eyes widen. I'm drenched head to toe in blood, my eyes must be golden, and electricity sparks off me into a plethora of colourful sparks.

Strolling towards him, a sick thrill crawls up my spine as he wets himself and whimpers like a beaten puppy. I grasp his curly blonde hair and pull his head back, exposing his neck to me. Using my free right hand, that still grasps the kitchen knife, I press the silver blade against his throat, causing his skin to hiss and turn an angry red.

Victor is begging and screaming like the little boy had been. He did not heed him – why should I? Slicing the blade across his carotid artery, he chokes and I release him. Allowing him to drop to the ground on his back, while he continues to choke on his own blood.

Using my magic, I make the blood coating my body evaporate and step closer, to the dying form of Victor.

"Your time is over," I utter, unnatural power vibrating through my voice. "You lost, and no one will mourn you."

"Fuck...you," Victor chokes out, blood dribbling down his lips. "Fuck – you all."

I smile, a cruel smile. "If that's how you feel, you can die alone."

He loses consciousness as I march over to the plump little boy and scoop him up into my arms. His fearful innocent eyes stare up at me. He's so small and young.

"You're safe now," I promise. "I'll take you to safety."

He weeps joyfully in response, his little arms wrapping around my neck in gratitude. I glance behind me to look at Victor, he isn't breathing – he's dead. My mission is accomplished.

I am the predator. I am a killer. I am a winner. Yet, I am forever changed.

It was easy killing them, there was no challenge, no danger, no risk of losing. I knew they couldn't win; I knew they would die; I knew I am the ultimate predator. Half-werewolf, half-vampire and with powerful magic. There is nothing I can't do or kill. I know if I wanted to, I could become a dark, dangerous creature. I could wipe out Henri and my father's forces. Maybe I should. Though, if I did. I would be just like them.

CHAPTER XXIII

The plump little boy was reunited with his parents, a small beacon of light in a period of darkness. It was a miracle to behold. Two parents hugging their son. I did not stay long in the clearing, as Melody and I needed to talk – alone. Still do. Melody looks at me anxiously. We stand on the nexus-point of the ley lines, formerly known as the meadow with the wildflowers.

JJ was taking a nap when I informed Liam about what I did. Once JJ wakes up, it will be Liam's turn to sleep – a sleep-deprived Alpha is no help to anyone. Liam was surprised and a fraction upset to hear the news that I killed Victor, who was his ex-best friend and ex-lover, though he admitted, it is a big win for us. Victor was a dangerous weapon on the enemy's side.

Melody is hugging herself, her heart rate erratic. She did not survive the genocides whole. Her left arm ends in a stump, where her hand had been previously. Melody was discussing something with Nicky when I asked to chat privately. Nicky looked well enough, a leather eyepatch over his injured eye, hiding the scars and empty socket.

"We should begin," I deadpan. "Before it starts really snowing."

A flurry of snow is descending, our exhales of breath coming in the forms of mist. Melody nods and hugs herself tighter. She is wearing a bloodied hoodie, leggings and trainers. Overall, not the best clothing in today's frigid temperature.

She sniffs, her voice trembling. "What do you want to know?"

"Can you see everything without the haze now Victor is dead?"

"Yes, my Sight is clear." An expression of sorrow is on her face. "I wish I could have seen the attacks coming. I feel responsible, for I could have saved them all if Victor hadn't been involved."

I share her guilt; I could have stopped it from happening. If only I had killed Father or Victor, or if I had not come here. I am the one to blame. The bitch was right. There are many things I could've done that would've saved them. Now all that is left of three former packs is 105 survivors.

"Will more survivors arrive?" I enquire.

"No. The little boy you found was the last one out there. You are his guardian angel."

My lips twitch, he called me that to his parents – his guardian angel. There was a newfound respect and admiration in people's eyes when I returned him and uttered the statement – *I killed Victor.*

Part of me wonders if I should end this fight, kill every single vampire and packless who follows Father and Henri.

"Don't," Melody whispers, approaching me, her right hand gripping my shoulder. "You don't want to do what I did. I thought it would make me feel better, that it would protect those I loved. Yet, by committing that act, I embraced a darkness inside me that has never gone away, a darkness that makes me unworthy of those I care about."

"I'm not like you, Melody." I push her hand off my shoulder and step back. "I know I'm not a monster. I know that killing is necessary, and I know I have what it takes to not be impacted by it."

"Bullshit, killing changes you."

"It does," I agree. "Nevertheless, it has not driven me to the belief that I'm unlovable or undeserving of love."

"You will if you cross that line."

"What's the alternative then?"

"If Henri Dupont and Thomas Blake are killed, their forces will retreat."

"How can you think of letting the majority of them go? Your mother is dead." She flinches back. "Theon's father is dead." She flinches backwards again. "And I know Cathy is in a coma, unlikely ever to wake up." A tear creeps down her face. "That's where your soulmate is, sitting next to his cousin, praying to the Goddess that she'll wake up."

"Revenge isn't always the answer," Melody retorts weakly.

"Says the girl who had her revenge." She looks down, ashamed. "So, the options are, I kill Henri and my father, let their forces go, or massacre all of them, or wait for them to attack us."

Melody nods and I grit my teeth. If I wait for them to attack, their deaths are justified and aren't solely killed by myself. Except, there could be casualties on my side. What if Liam, Tegan, JJ or any of my pack members got hurt?

Should I cross the line and become like my foes, someone who can commit genocide? No, I'll wait for them to attack. I won't be them.

"That's an okay choice too," Melody states, without me having to tell her my decision.

"They will die, regardless."

"Yes, but their deaths won't rest solely on you."

A brief silence befalls us. I know I can't trust her, not fully, not like I have. She didn't tell me about the bitch. What else does she know that she hasn't told me? I can tell Melody knows what I'm thinking. What I will ask. It seems to make her more anxious. She hugs her body once more. What secrets is she hiding?

"I can't tell you what you seek," Melody says abruptly. "If I tell you what I know, it will impact the future. Sometimes it is necessary to withhold information to ensure a better outcome."

"Who made you the judge?"

"The Goddess."

"Fuck her, I deserve to know. What are you holding back about my life?" I take a deep breath and ask, "And, why didn't you tell me that my aunt was a blood purist, who had been hunting me!?"

146

"It wasn't important."

My magic surges out of me, slamming Melody onto the ground. "The bitch had her hand inside my chest, ready to rip my heart out. She made me think she accepted me like Mum. Do you know what it is like to be hated by your own blood?" She shakes her head. "No, I didn't think so. It is a shitty feeling. Now I'm going to give you a choice. You either tell me what else you've been hiding, or I penetrate your mind and learn it the hard way."

"Please, Clay. I will tell you soon, but once everything is sorted."

"No, I need to know. And knowing you, you may be willing to sacrifice your life in the coming fight."

"Clay please, I'm begging you—"

I will never hear the rest of what she was going to say, as my magic penetrates her mind and I'm flung inside her memories. It is different to the time I penetrated Liam's mind, so I could share my memories with him. This time, I'm searching for forbidden knowledge inside someone else's head, while the owner tries to push me out. Which is an impossible task, my magic is burrowed deep, and my intention is unwavering. I need to know what she is keeping from me.

Initially, I thought maybe not telling me about the bitch's intentions was an oversight. However, she made it crystal-clear that it was deliberate, and she is keeping other secrets too. Which apparently, will impact my future if I know about it. I don't care, I need to know what she is hiding.

It is hard to cling to one memory. Most fly too fast to comprehend. Although a name echoes in her mind: Ian. Who is Ian, and why does she feel guilty about it? Discarding the unimportant information, I focus, willing the memories to slow, and despite some resistance, Melody's mind obeys.

The first memory I can cling to is of Melody at fifteen or fourteen. Her hair flows all the way to her waist, and she sits at a vanity table, brushing her hair as eyes that hold a multitude of loneliness, stare blankly into the vanity's mirror. The door to her room opens, revealing a man with black hair and skin like snow. Melody's eyes light up a fraction at seeing him, as if seeing a glass of water in a vast desert.

I instantly see the resemblance to Victor; they share the same bone structure. This is his father, Alpha Drake, standing in the doorway. Ominous red eyes glare down at Melody.

"Father," Melody calls in greeting. "Having a good day?"

"No," he hisses. "There was an attack, and you didn't tell me."

"I didn't see," Melody whimpers, dropping her brush and standing. "Forgive me, Father."

"I forgive you. Except, my forgiveness comes with a price – you must be punished."

"I know."

I push the memory away, the moment he strikes her, my heart aches painfully. This was a mistake. I've crossed a boundary; I should not have. Pulling myself out of her mind and retracting my magic, I look down at Melody, silent tears streaming down her face.

"Promise me," I croak. "That you will tell me what you are hiding, and you will be alive to do so."

"I swear it on Theon's life," Melody sniffs as she gets up and wipes her tears.

"I'm sorry," I apologise, bringing her into a hug. Her arms encircle my midsection, and she sobs. Guilt claws at me. I made her relive that moment – being a captive, being scared of her kidnapper, whom it seems, she was forced to call Father.

Whatever she is withholding can wait until the looming danger is exterminated. Then, I will know. I just hope whatever she is keeping from me won't forever fracture our friendship.

CHAPTER XXIV

I discussed my theory about what a sacred werewolf bite might do to a human with Melody, as we walked back to the clearing. She agreed to talk to Tegan and offer her the bite, though Melody would not tell me if it would work. Who knows? Maybe Melody doesn't know either.

Upon returning, Erin and Nicky roped me into setting traps around the clearing—magical ones that will prove fatal to any enemy who means harm. To set up the traps was a mixture of rune work and incantations. The incantations were rather simple, but I struggled to correctly draw the rune sequences. Erin had to double check my work.

As we did this, an Omega looked after Cordelia, whom the Parry siblings have unofficially adopted as their own.

I needed blood urgently half way through setting the traps. Like all I could think about was the sweet nectar that flows in ones' body. Nicky allowed himself to be my brunch, and it was a bit awkward afterwards.

When we return to the protection of the force field, it's midday, and an inch or two of snow has settled onto the ground, as well as a light coating on the buildings and trees.

The cold did not bother us as we worked, since Nicky knew an incantation that can keep one's body temperature lovely and toasty— a spell Maeve, his *wee younger sister,* taught him.

Without that advantage, I'm impressed to see pack warriors continuing to patrol along the metal fence, guarding the clinic and the entrance to the pack house.

As I stroll to the log cabin, Nicky and Erin hurriedly disappear into the pack house to find Cordelia. Once in view, I'm mildly surprised to see two pack warriors guarding the log cabin's door. They both greet me, and one opens the door, letting me step inside. Liam is not asleep, he's at his desk working. It looks so mundane, unlike what I've been doing today and yesterday.

We haven't talked, not really, not since I apologised for telekinetically shoving him. Or the night we told each other we loved one another. Both events feel like lifetimes ago. The door closing draws Liam's attention. His stormy grey orbs examine me.

If I met my past-self, the one who had not met Melody Morning, my past-self would see a stranger. I've changed so much: I have magic, my appearance is different, I don't wonder if I'm an abomination and I have someone I love.

My Alpha-boy will always be the single most important thing in my life. Speaking of him, he leaves his desk, sauntering towards me, his tight dark tee and jeans, scandalously showing off his sex appeal. Part of me can't believe Liam is my man.

He halts in front of me, his face tilted upwards, to look me in the eyes. "I've missed you."

"Me too. The nap did you some good," I whisper, and our lips collide, his calloused hands clutching the hoodie I stole from his closet. We have not been alone together in over twenty-four hours. Pulling back, I ask, "Do you need to work?"

"No, I'm waiting on a few emails from a few packs we have alliances with. Supposedly if any pack is under severe threat, as we are, the allied packs are meant to come running. Although, I doubt they'll come or arrive in time."

"What about the Werewolf Council?"

"Useless." Liam sneers, our soul bond pooling full of righteous fury. "Their representative said they might be able to send one or two of their government sanctioned warriors to our aid in a week's time. Except, we would be dead by then or victorious."

"We will be victorious. There is no, or, it is a fact."

"How can you be so certain?"

"Because, you have me."

"You?"

"Yes, me. When I killed Victor, I took out three vampires and two Deltas first. None of them had a chance to attack me—I'm that powerful. I even considered attacking my father and Henri's forces alone."

"I forbid that to ever happen," Liam states. "That is too dangerous, no matter the power someone wields."

"Like I said, I considered it. I'm not doing it, as I'm not like them. I cannot commit genocide. I might be able to accomplish it, but I won't do it."

"If I had your strength, I'm not sure I would say the same," Alpha-boy admits. "I want my revenge on Henri, very badly, I will be the one to kill him, and it won't be a quick or easy death."

I cup Liam's face as tears glimmer in his eyes. "I know we have not talked about it since the first time. Nevertheless, you can talk about what happened to your parents and brothers with me."

"I know I can—I'm just ashamed. They might be alive if we hadn't gone on a picnic that day. The only reason I survived was that I left to pee at the right time." Shamefully, he swipes his tears away, our soul bond a storm of emotions. "Soon after I left to pee, I smelt blood and heard fighting, so I ran back to the pack house and got help. By the time we arrived back, my brothers and mom were dead, their remains scattered about everywhere." Liam takes a deep breath and continues. "Henri Dupont was the only packless in human form, and I recognised him, as he was the known leader of the attacks. I can still vividly hear his laughter as he beat my dad to death. That day was his last attack. He had done what he had set out to do."

"What does that mean?"

"Henri Dupont was once a member of Willow pack, many years ago in my parents' youth," Liam reveals. "His soulmate rejected Henri as she was in love with my dad, and when my dad refused her advances, because he was happily mated to my mom, she vanished and was never seen again. Henri blamed everyone, especially my parents, and he fled. Most assumed his destination was his native pack in France. Though before fleeing, he promised he would one day return for vengeance."

"And he did."

"He did," Liam agrees tonelessly as he buries his face in the crook of my neck, sobbing as his arms hold me tight against his body. Memories of the worst day of my life surface in my head. *Run, my sweet boy, run.* And I did. I ran so far, I'm on a flipping different continent to where I was born.

I believe if Mum were alive, she would have loved Liam, and if Liam's parents had been alive, I think they would have loved me too. Except, we will never know. My father and Henri Dupont took that opportunity away. All because of Father's bigotry and Henri's soulmate, who did not want him.

Sniffing, Liam looks up at me, his eyes shining red. "I love you, Clay. More than I thought possible—marry me."

For a brief moment, I wonder if he is joking. Then Liam releases me, falls to one knee, and produces a gold ring out of his pocket. We've known each other for five days. An insane person would agree to marry someone in that time frame.

I open my mouth to say no but I just know in that split second, I can't. My love is more than any human could love someone in a lifetime. There will be no one else. When he passes to the next world, I will remain, and my heart will never find this love again.

"Yes," I whisper, my voice trembling with emotion. "I'll marry you. You're my world. My soulmate. The one love of my eternal life. You are my Alpha-boy."

Liam laughs gleefully, tears of happiness flowing down his face. He slips the ring onto my finger and slams his lips onto mine while simultaneously lifting me into the air.

I will remain with him as time weathers his appearance. But to me, he shall forever be young, my Alpha-boy. Placing me down, our lips' part, and I know that the coming danger will pass, that we will survive. That our pack will too.

"Meeting you," Liam chokes back a sob. "Was the best day of my life."

"Mine too," I confess, and our lips once more seal together. I don't care what I have to do. I would set cities ablaze to protect Liam. The darkness inside me whispers that I should sneak away, so I can eradicate Father and Henri and all their followers. I won't, because if Liam ever saw me as a monster or an abomination—I would be unable to live with myself.

~

Liam's calloused fingers glide through my hair, his other hand typing lazily on his laptop, responding to important emails. We lie on the bed, my head resting on his lap. The laptop is to Liam's right, his main focus. There is peacefulness. How I wish this could go on forever. It won't, we have time, yet it won't last.

A handful of pack members have come into our blissful haven, asking questions and discussing important matters. The most important matter discussed is the brave pack warriors, who stalk our enemies' movements and report back. They believe it is only a matter of time until Father's and Henri's forces will attack. Luckily, our enemies believe Victor has run away like a coward, not knowing he's been killed.

On a more positive note, those who entered probably saw our engagement rings. So, news of our engagement will be known and spread quickly—a happy Alpha and Alpha-Male, makes for a happy pack.

I twist my engagement ring, it is a simple gold ring with an inscription on the exterior, *Forever Mine*. The engagement ring is a Willow family heirloom, to be given to the Alpha's counterpart. An enchantment must be on it to fit me perfectly.

Liam has an almost identical engagement ring on, it is also a Willow family heirloom. His is different, as on the exterior of his ring are the words, *My Heart's Desire*. A true statement. My heart will always desire him. Liam catches me gazing up at his face and smiles gently. A wave of affection filling our soul bond, his important email forgotten.

"I did not know I would love someone like this. It swallows me whole, it is all-encompassing," Liam states matter-of-factly. "Two days ago, when you died in that meadow, those ten seconds you were dead, were enough for me to know I wanted to marry you." Liam ceases running his fingers through my hair. "I was going to ask you, in the evening the next day. Unfortunately, everything happened and my plans were foiled. I know it wasn't a romantic proposal. I apologise for that. I just couldn't go another second without a ring on your finger."

I grin. "The proposal doesn't matter. What matters is our love."

"You're right," Liam agrees. "Though when I think of our wedding, and I do look forward to it, it hurts to think that my parents and brothers won't be there. They were so supportive when I came out. My eldest brother, Peter, threw this gigantic coming out party. A few traditionalists couldn't take the idea of a homosexual leading them one day, and left. Yet no one, not a single individual, ever blamed me."

"That's beautiful," I mumble, sorrow and regret oozing into our soul bond. "I didn't get the chance to tell my mum that I liked guys—I regret that every day. She was a great woman; she didn't deserve to live in fear as we did. Part of me can't understand why she chose me over her soulmate."

"I believe any mother would choose their child over their significant other, even if they were their soulmate," Liam suggests as he closes his laptop and places it on the bedside table. A few moments later, he pushes my head off his lap and moves until he is lying horizontally next to me on the bed. He brings a sturdy arm around me comfortingly, his stormy grey eyes never looking away from me. His eyes are my favourite shade of grey.

When it is just the two of us, it's like the world outside doesn't exist, or the world could end, and we wouldn't notice. The idea of choosing someone over my Alpha is impossible. I press a timid kiss against Liam's mouth, he quirks his lips into a smirk and returns my affection with a passionate snog.

We are soulmates. We are fiancés. We are in love.

"They will be coming soon," I utter, the words poisonous to say. "We could be hurt or die, not that I would let either happen. Though despite what I say, this could be our last time together."

"It could," Liam agrees. "And we could also lose many friends and pack members. What is your point?"

"My point is that we are in love, soulmates and engaged. We have a slither of time left. Do you not desire to be physical with me at least once?"

"I would like nothing more than to take you right here and now. Except, I won't. I made a promise to you that our first time would be amazing, romantic, and all our dangers would be behind us."

I snort. "And I said the last one was slightly unrealistic."

"You did. Still, I will be keeping my promise. An incentive for both of us to survive."

"We will survive, I shouldn't have doubted it. And if anything were to happen," it pains me to think of his demise. "Not a thing in this universe would stop me, in moving heaven and earth to save you."

"Nor me, I would do the same."

I chuckle quietly. "Except, between the two of us, I might actually be able to move heaven and earth."

"You are a powerful force, proven too—when you killed Victor."

I bite my lip. "I know you two were close. It's okay to be upset that he's dead."

"I don't mourn Victor," Alpha-boy scoffs. "I mourn the person he pretended to be, the person who comforted me at my weakest. I have a ton of fond memories, though, they are nothing compared to the type of person Victor was—a monster."

"He was," I agree, thinking of how pathetic he was in his last moments. He deserved it. Our lips meet again in a chaste kiss, his free calloused hand stroking my cheek.

There will most likely be deaths on both sides, mainly our enemies. Unfortunately, some pack members will die too. A choice I made, as I did not desire to sink to the level of our enemies. Would I come to regret this? Possibly. And I will live with it. Yes. I won't run or repress my emotions like Melody. Killing and death are unavoidable...

CHAPTER XXV

Loud knocks disperse our tranquillity. Liam and I roll out of bed in unison, and I reach the door first, swinging it open to reveal JJ. His clothing is rumpled and curly blonde hair askew. Without speaking a word, he pivots and sprints towards the training grounds. We follow quickly behind. JJ pauses next to a group of pack members who are gawking at a sweaty Tegan, clad in her underwear, on all fours, her hair plastered to her skin. The snow around her has melted into a puddle of steaming water. I know the cause instantly; a bite mark is visible on her left forearm.

Melody serenely observes the situation, while Erin and Nicky stand either side of her, also with an air of calm. Dylan and Theon are among the onlookers.

The thrum of blood songs fills my ears momentarily, allowing me to hear that Tegan's blood song is altering to that of werewolf. She is changing—a sacred werewolf bite really does change a human into a werewolf.

"What's going on?" Liam frowns, several pack members mumbling the same question.

"Melody has bitten Tegan," I reply. "And she is in the process of becoming a werewolf."

His eyes widen comically, and I stifle a laugh. JJ furiously stomps towards Melody and begins arguing with her. Melody's responses are relaxed and vague. Is there a chance Tegan could die? Probably.

This is a dangerous transformation. Every cell in her body is changing.

My thoughts, and the arguing between Melody and JJ, are forgotten as Tegan releases a deafening scream that propels her head back. Gasps arise as Tegan's irises and pupils vanish, leaving her eyes void of colour.

Gradually, a light dusting of black fur sprouts on her olive skin. Quivering, she releases a wail, a wail a banshee would be proud of— if they were real. Tegan whimpers, shredding the underwear off herself, as she convulses and contorts, bones snapping and reshaping, her face elongating, and teeth growing too big for her human mouth. In seconds, a huge black furred wolf with white patches is in Tegan's place.

"She has survived the transformation," Melody announces. Tegan huffs, her eerie blank eyes surveying everyone. JJ tentatively approaches his soulmate, his eyes shining purple. Tegan growls, her haunches raised as if JJ would attack her. He kneels on the training ground's wet tarmac, one hand caressing her neck, the other raised in a harmless gesture. Carefully, he bares his throat. Tegan whines and pushes her snout into the conjunction of JJ's throat and shoulder, inhaling his scent. Many look away at such an intimate act, an act I will never perform with Liam.

A confusing amount of jealousy is born inside me. I told Melody my theory and asked her to offer Tegan the bite. I did this, so why is this making me feel such jealousy? Then I realise why—Tegan isn't an outcast anymore. *I'm alone again.* No, I'm not, I have Liam. *You won't one day.* Willing the urge to cry away, I step back, stumbling towards the log cabin. *Alone.* They are all too absorbed in Tegan transformation to notice my departure. Locking the door behind me, I shut my eyes. *How will you feel when you are alone once more? It is only a matter of time. Everyone could die today. Or everyone you care about shall be dead in a century. What's the difference?* What is the difference?

I shiver and open my burning eyes. I've changed so much: my appearance, my supernatural powers and my morality. Would past-me approve of what I've become? Would Mum? The answer is unknown.

Mum didn't raise a killer, she raised a fearful boy, who didn't know how to throw a punch—she didn't prepare me for this prey or predator world.

Enough! I am who I am. These past two years and eight days have made a better, stronger, and more powerful version of myself. Eight days or two years ago, I would have been unable to stand tall, ready to face a legion of packless and vampires. I would not be able to face my father.

Unlocking the door, I meander outside. The sky has darkened—a storm is coming. It will wash away the snow and blood to be spilled. The sick perverse hunger reawakens inside me. The deserving will perish. A chorus of blood songs approach. Thunder sounds. Someone shouts, and a howl echoes in the air. One of the magical traps is triggered, causing an explosion. They are here.

A blast of green light strikes against the force field, and within seconds the magical barrier is gone—they have found a magic user. My magic swirls out of me, coating my skin, rendering me invisible. It is time for the predator to hunt again. I have to kill Father. I have to be the one, like Liam has to be the one to kill Henri. Mum deserves vengeance, and so do the victims of the genocides. Raising my hands, I sense that my nails have become claws, blood will drip from them soon.

Among the chaos of running pack members, and Liam yelling orders, I see Melody. Her liquid moonlight eyes, gazing at me. She gives a subtle nod. Another magical trap goes off, causing a booming explosion. This is it—the battle of life and death.

I need a magic boost. Stretching my consciousness, I connect to the ley lines, their magic and strength pooling into me. There will be no survivors on our enemies' side. That's a promise. Sprinting, I head towards the danger and leap atop the metal fence, somehow manging to keep a balance. The sole person who is aware of me is Melody—

her eyes following me. Our gazes lock again, fleetingly. Some days ago, she was my saviour—now, I am my own saviour.

Looking away, I stare at Liam. He's in his element, his deep voice commanding and authoritative as he gives his orders. JJ is giving him back up, and I swear if he survives, I'll ask what JJ stands for.

Tegan is still in wolf form next to JJ, and I know she will fight. That she won't stay hidden. She wanted to do more, and I've given her that option.

I can't see Dylan; he's probably finding Jared and Katie. Theon is gone too, most likely to protect his comatose cousin.

The Parry siblings next to Melody are standing tall and scanning the tree-lines, electricity waltzing against their ebony skin. It will take a while for our enemies to trigger or avoid all the magical traps to reach the clearing. Though when they do, death will greet them. Dropping down, I disappear into the woods, my second hunt has officially begun.

CHAPTER XXVI

Magical traps are triggered left and right. Screams and howls of agony reverberate through the world. There is no sunlight, as storm clouds have blocked the sun out. I suspect the magic user has summoned the storm. Sheets of rain bombard everywhere, washing blood and snow away.

I pause walking, staring down at a dying packless woman. Her legs and arms are broken. Several wide wounds are prolific across her body, a constant stream of blood flowing out of them. One of the magical traps did this. Mercifully, I break her neck, her life and pain gone.

I continue on, discovering dead and dying individuals. I can't be merciful to them all. The magical traps were a good idea. By the time all of them are triggered, or when they've learned to avoid them, the enemy forces will be severely depleted.

Abruptly and luckily, I pivot at the last second, narrowly avoid triggering a magical trap. Just what I need. To be blown in half.

Sneaking past a handful of vampires, I observe the anxiety coming off them in waves, and one of them is mumbling about deserting. We didn't consider that the magical traps might make our enemies consider fleeing.

Leaping over a root, I crouch, seeing a forty-something warlock. His slitted pupils are green, his irises ultramarine and his sclerae a pale yellow. He's chanting in the lyrical language of magic. *"Rise, your work is not done. Rise, to avenge your death. Rise, to finish your task."*

He repeats the three sentences over and over. I wonder what the spell will do. The Goddess answers my question as I notice a corpse of a vampire with only half its body remaining, start twitching, and moving while its eyes dart side to side—necromancy. He's making the dead continue to fight.

My hunt for Father can wait. This warlock will perish first.

I creep towards my new prey, his chanting continues, unaware of the danger headed to him. Why is he helping Henri and Father? Is it money? I want to know the answer. My magic penetrates his mind. It's harder to do, like a force field had been protecting it, although my magic still is able to penetrate his mind.

The warlock collapses to his knees, no longer chanting. I telekinetically hold him down, his mind is unremarkable, though his wealth of magical knowledge will be useful. Apparently, what I'm doing is called mind magic, a subcategory of wordless magic. The warlock's name is Brandon West, he's forty-eight, has no family, kids or soulmate. He has lived a life of offering his magic for money. Many innocent lives have been lost, because he chose money over people, and the world will be better without him in it.

"Please," Brandon pleads. "I don't want to die."

No one ever does. I burrow deeper into his mind, then lash out. Brandon weeps and screams, as brain matter dribbles out of the orifices on his face.

Retracting from his mind, I know the damage is done. Releasing him from my magic, Brandon topples backwards, his eyes dashing left and right. He can't see me; my invisibility has remained.

Pitifully, Brandon inhales and inhales, unable to exhale, he can't remember how. I can also smell urine and faeces, his bladder and bowel control forgotten. Glancing away, I see the undead half vampire corpse, dragging itself towards the clearing. I know the counter to the necromancy spell, thanks to Brandon's memories. I can't be bothered to wait for him to die. *"Rest, your work is done. Rest, your vengeance is over. Rest, your task is finished."*

The counterspell takes effect after the fifth time I chant it. The half vampire corpse stops, once again, just a corpse. Sensing someone, I tense and side-step, narrowly avoiding a packless Gamma. Dropping my invisibility, I lunge at her, my claws deeply raking across her hairline, her right eye and all the way to her jaw. Whimpering, she cups her face, stumbling backwards, and hits the ground hard after tripping over the half vampire corpse.

Directing my magic, my attempted attacker bursts into flames, her screams joining the cacophony of wails and howls. Sensing someone else, I whirl around and spot a male vampire, a mask of terror on his face. He looks a year or so younger than me. I notice it is no longer raining, and the storm clouds have dissipated. Brandon must be dead.

The vampire, rather than face me, steps back into the sunlight behind him. His body catching on fire instantaneously. He doesn't scream, his red eyes remain on me. He was weak prey.

Allowing my magic to coat my skin again, I become invisible as I continue my hunt.

Regrettably, after a few minutes, I stumble into a small field that contains about thirty packless in wolf form. Their senses are more heightened in this form, and thus, their Gamma and Delta eyes land on me. Sighing bitterly, I drop my invisibility again and attack, shooting fire and electricity out of my hands, all the while dodging a barrage of attempted attacks. Somehow, there is tranquillity in killing and an additive rush.

The wise packless, realising they are no match, flee with their tails between their legs, only to trigger a magical trap. Their bodies are torn apart by the resulting explosion.

As I move the dead into a pile, I take a second to take everything in. I'm not ashamed of what I've done. It is me or them, and none of them are innocent. How many innocents did they kill during the genocides?

Sighing again, I ponder what I should do? Father could be

anywhere. He could be dead already, one of the countless victims of the magical traps. But, no, he's too smart to die like that. I'll lure him to me.

Raising my hands, I blast bolts of electricity into the air, high above the treetops, and into the cloudless sky. Minutes pass before some vampires and packless come to investigate. Their lives are quickly ended, joining the pile of dead. Screams, howls, and explosions don't fill the world as they did previously.

Straining, I hear the sound of combat, probably originating from the clearing. I hope the enemy forces have been weakened. Severely weakened, and that we have set up an adequate number of magical traps.

A slow condescending clapping snaps me out of my thoughts. Whirling towards the source, I lower my arms. Tendrils of electricity wrapping around my hands and forearms. The source of the clapping is—my father, Thomas Blake. His three-piece suit is coated in blood and grime, his bowler hat is missing, blood covers his hands, but somehow his face is immaculate and hair is still in place.

"Aren't you kill happy?" Father drawls, his eyes looking at the pile of dead, his bloodstained hands continuing clapping together condescendingly. "You've changed so much. I hardly see the scared little coward who ran when mummy yelled for him to go."

Run, my sweet boy, run. No. I don't run anymore. I am a predator. *So, is he.* I know that, I see it in his eyes.

We circle each other, and I try to immobilise him with my magic. He laughs, unaffected, and raises his right hand. On his thumb is a ring covered in runes. "This is a special ring. It has some limited protection against magic. You'll find cheating quite hard."

"I will win anyway," I reply, my voice steady.

"Aren't you a confident brat?"

"I am," I agree as I throw bolts of electricity at him. Father dodges lazily, yawning. I try again, same result. His reflexes are faster than the fools I've faced. My confidence wavers, can I really win? *You can do anything, my sweet boy.*

Mum told me that when I was seven, and I wanted to play the piano, not kill her ex-soulmate, though the context is the same. I can do anything, I put my mind to.

CHAPTER XXVII

I block Father's punch, fall back and direct a gust of wind at him, knocking him on his back. Beads of sweat roll down my face, the taste of it is bitter in my mouth. He leaps to his feet and lunges again, his fist connecting with my jaw. Retreating, I spit blood out of my mouth. Father cackles. I shout an incantation, a powerful arc of blue fire, jetting out of both my palms.

The spell was not worthwhile, Father again dodging the attack. My magic is depleting fast, and I'm becoming fatigued. He's trying to tire me out, I realise, a genius plan.

"Getting tired, little coward?" Father says, a vicious smile on his lips. "You aren't looking so good."

I snarl and stomp my foot. The ground trembles, giving birth to several fissures. Father laughs and pounces, his fists slamming into my rib cage, one after the other, before backing away. The damage is done, he's broken my ribs, causing my vision to blur.

Cursing, I wonder how I, a hybrid with magic, can be losing. Grinding my teeth, I use my magic to aid my healing, as I try to ignore the intense pain.

In no time, my ribs are repaired to tip-top shape. Father growls and I avoid his next attack. Luckily, I deliver a kick to his left leg, shattering one of his bones. He swears obnoxiously loud. He's limping now as we circle one another. I'm unaware of how long we've been fighting—it feels like hours.

I dive at him, attempting to punch his smug face. He easily blocks, batting my feeble punch away, like a pro. Swearing, I evade his counterattack. I can't beat him in hand-to-hand-combat. I couldn't even punch him.

Evading another attack, I try to blast him with scalding hot water. He gracefully somersaults over it. Childishly, I attempt to punch him again, but like last time, he bats the punch away. Though unlike last time, he pulls my arm out of its socket.

Stumbling backwards in self-preservation, I pop my arm back into its socket. Despite my fast-dwindling reserves of magic, it is the only solution. Racking my brain for an incantation. One hits me.

"They mistreat you Mother Earth, swallow him whole," I utter, stomping my feet, and splitting open a chasm, devouring those I killed. Unfortunately, Father, out of pure fucking luck, manages to evade joining their fate.

Snarling, I know I'm minutes away from being out of magic. I may be faster and stronger than Father, but I am not skilled in combat like him. My confidence wavers again. *I can do anything, I set my mind to,* I remind myself. *Anything.*

"You will lose, little coward," Father taunts. "There's no one here to save you!"

"Shut the fuck up!"

I dive at him again, and finally land a punch on his smug face. He swears, striking me pettily back. Focusing my magic, the air around us condenses and rams him backwards. As he stumbles back, I deliver a kick to his chest, propelling him further towards the chasm. Father gasps, steadying himself on the edge. All it will take is one tiny shove. His eyes widen and he knows it is over. That's he lost.

"Son," his voice quivers pathetically. "I'll leave you alone, I promise."

"Are you really going to quit? After being part of three genocides, and leading your clan to doom?" He doesn't respond. "You have become the coward."

He sneers and tilts his head up snobbishly. "Do it then. Kill your own Father."

"You've never been my father. All you've ever done is bring ruin and pain. I won't miss you—you killed my mum. Goodbye, Thomas."

"Wait—" he gasps as I spring on him, slamming my knee into his gut. Gravity happily takes him. He screams, and Lady Luck smiles on him yet again. His fingers somehow clutch onto the edge. His pupils blown wide, and his terror is palpable. "Son, my boy. I'm sorry about everything. Please save me," he pleads, stupidly. "I'll help you. I can get the fighting to stop."

"Haven't I already said goodbye?" I snort, stomping on his right hand, smirking at the satisfying crunch. His right arm falls to his side, and all that holds him from certain death is his quivering left hand.

"Clay!"

I freeze, my foot hovers above his remaining hand. He has never called me that – not ever.

"Maria, your mum, she's alive. I swear it's true, I swear on all that is holy, I swear on my soul, I swear on the Goddess–Maria is alive! Pull me up and I'll take you to her. She's missed you so much." Sincerity fills his eyes.

Placing my foot down next to his hand, he smiles, red eyes twinkling in relief. I could discover if he's telling the truth if I penetrate his mind with my magic. Although, the idea of knowing his inner workings makes me nauseous. *Run, my sweet boy, run.* Tears pool in my eyes. Crouching, I offer my hand, and he lifts his broken hand to me.

"Maria will be the happiest woman in the world, when she sees you. We can be one big happy family—"

The moment our hands connect, he gasps, convulsing as electricity blazes throughout his body. His hand lets go of the edge and I drop him, watching dispassionately as he screams, falling to his doom, darkness consuming him. His screams will be a sound I'll always treasure. I can't take the chance he'll survive, so I mumble the counterspell and smirk as the chasm seals shut, becoming a barely noticeable fissure.

He's dead. Thomas Blake is dead.

He will not be missed. That man was a liar, a racist, and one of the masterminds behind three genocides. *You should have not been born.* Those were his first words to me, and his last words to me were complete bullshit, *we can be one big happy family.* I hadn't been a hundred percent sure if he was lying, however, the moment he uttered those words, I knew he was speaking a load of shit.

Standing, I jog back to the clearing, avoiding magical traps and using my magic to make me invisible again. The metal fences that surrounded the clearings have been knocked down. Pack warriors fight against the invading force. They all seem so heroic.

Though the Parry siblings seem especially heroic, weaving through the fighting, healing and setting enemies on fire.

Of course, my eyes eventually find themselves on my Alpha-boy, who is coated in blood and naked as the day he was born. He is up against an ugly rat-faced man. This has to be Henri Dupont.

My focus is diverted to someone screaming, JJ. He cradles one of his arms, his metal staff is discarded on the ground. I'm about to intervene when Tegan pounces, shredding the vampire like paper. Everything is in hand. Our enemies are losing and outnumbered. Victory is in the air.

Smiling, I join the affray. Slashing and punching, killing and injuring. They are the prey; we are the predators. Dropping my invisibility for the third time today, I deal a death blow to a packless who almost raked his claws across Melody's face.

"Thanks," she breathes out. I nod and we fight side by side. Their numbers are thinning fast. Some dare to flee, but are chased down. There will be no survivors. I had promised that after all.

Tegan leaps over me, shredding a wolf behind me. I shout thank you and side-step a punch, pivot and yank out the offender's heart. Gasping, my knees buckle, and I look behind my shoulder to witness JJ's metal staff impaling, a vampire through her heart. I nod at JJ in thanks, he nods back. I have never felt closer to my pack as I fight alongside them, nor will I ever feel as close as I do now.

Pushing myself to my feet, I diverge from my comrades, coming to Liam's aid by throwing a ball of fire at Henri. He swears and flips backwards, evading the fireball.

That bastard was about to land a possibly mortal wound on MY LIAM! My magic lashes out, pinning him to the ground.

"You, okay?" Liam asks casually.

"I am," I confirm.

"Is your father dead?"

"He is no father of mine. He is just an extremely dead vampire."

"Good," he chuckles, and Liam approaches Henri, who lies helpless on his back. This is the man who killed his parents and siblings. A man who doesn't deserve to live.

"This is for my mom and dad," Liam whispers. "For Peter and Freddie, and all the lives you helped take."

Liam doesn't give him any time to reply, his left foot descending down onto his face. Henri's head explodes like a fragile watermelon, thrown off a building. The sounds of battle have ended. Looking about, I see our enemies are dead. Victory really is ours.

My Alpha-boy strolls confidently towards me, cups my face and kisses me. We won, they are dead, the genocides are avenged, and our pack is safe. We are safe. We will get our lifetime together. More threats will arise, and we will face them together and win. We are predators, and we are the winners.

CHAPTER XXVIII

There were few fatalities on our side, but many injured, making the clinic busy again. I learned JJ's full name is Jericho Jenkins. He was my partner, as we hauled dead bodies into a pile to burn. Liam was spared the task, as he needed to contact the Werewolf Council and our allied packs to tell them that the threat is over. Erin and Nicky were also spared, given the dangerous task of deactivating the remaining magical traps.

During the hauling of the dead, JJ told me stories of Liam when they were younger, as well as how he became the Beta of the pack. His father was the Beta before him, and when he got injured in a packless attack, he handed the title over to JJ, who was sixteen at the time. To retain the title, he had to fight thirty-two pack warriors. JJ won, proving he deserved the honour of being the Beta.

Chatting with JJ was enjoyable, but the affair was cut short when Tegan shifted to her human form and fainted. JJ then accompanied her to the clinic. He wasn't worried, informing me it is normal to pass out after your first shift. I noticed Tegan's hair had streaks of white, a possible side-effect of being turned into a werewolf.

Once JJ left, Melody swooped to my side and whisked me away to the nexus-point to discuss what she wouldn't tell me earlier. Melody paces, her arms behind her back. She hasn't said a word since the clearing.

Biting my bottom lip, I ponder what she could be keeping from me. A long lost-sibling, or possibly that I'm not immortal. The latter is just hopeful thinking, I'm not confident I can stomach an eternity alone.

"What is it you're withholding?" I question.

Melody ceases to pace, a tired expression forming on her face. "Thomas was telling the truth—your mum is alive."

"That's not funny," I hiss, a heavy weight appearing in my throat, "you told me she died. That she wasn't given a quick death."

"I lied."

"You lied?!" I shout in disbelief, electricity sparking off my palms.

"She did die for a minute or two from the beating she received, but she lived. If you had known the truth, you'd have wanted to save her, and it always resulted in your death." Melody sighs and runs her hand through her hair. "Plus, Maria is under a spell. She can't remember you, believes herself human, and thinks Thomas is her human husband, who travels for work."

"You're not lying, are you?" I whisper, curling and unfurling my hands into fists.

"No."

"Where is she?" I demand, the urge to punch her is overwhelming.

"In a tiny village off the coast of Wales."

I want to be sick. "Is that it?" I snarl. "That one huge secret!?"

"No," Melody hesitates. "There is another."

My mind races through a thousand possibilities. "What is it!?"

"Sabrina, your ex," she swallows, fear filling her eyes. "She gave birth to a son, your son. I didn't tell you, because he would have been a distraction."

My knees buckle, thudding into the moist earth. The world feels upside down. Thomas was telling the truth. Mum is alive, and I have a son! Two things my seer "friend" knew, but didn't inform me. She's betrayed me. There is no other word for it.

She knew Mum was alive and lied. She knew I had a son and didn't tell me. I thought she was a friend. I wasn't—maybe all I ever was to her was a tool. A tool that would help her atone, and her reasoning to hide that I have a son is disgusting. *Distraction.*

As I gaze up at the woman who forever changed my life, I feel hatred. I will always be grateful yet, I won't ever trust her again. She knew I harboured colossal guilt over Mum's "death", and Melody could have stopped that by telling me the truth. How will I face Mum? I killed her twin and her ex-soulmate. She'll be disgusted by me.

Should I have spared Thomas? He was telling the truth? Then again, he probably would have killed me, if I had pulled him up to safety. Shaking my head, my thoughts careen onto my nameless son. And I recall being in Melody's mind, she was thinking of a name— Ian. Is that the name of my son?

"What," I choke back a sob, "is his name?"

"His name is Ian Green." I should have dug deeper; I would have found out then. "Ian's eighteen months old. His human side is dominant, and, at the moment, his supernatural abilities are dormant."

"So, my son's basically human." I sigh in relief; he won't have to know the hatred of being a hybrid.

"Yes," Melody agrees, "though his heritage will one day become active."

Bile rises in my throat. "Then Ian needs to be with me."

"He does," Melody confirms. "Sabrina and her parents have cared for him well. However, they can't protect him from those who will despise him for his impure blood, and you know that."

"Of course, I know he'll be despised!" I throw my hands onto the ground, causing a mini earthquake. It is unfair that Ian will face these prejudices. All because I'm his father. Sniffing, I enquire. "Does he have a connection to the Source?"

Melody nods. "He will be able to perform magic when he is older."

A type of hatred I never knew could exist, blooms inside me.

Thomas Blake, my sperm donor, cost me so much. I didn't get to see my son be born, or his first words, or his first steps. I will never get that back.

Mum may be restored to her former self; however, I will never get the time I lost. Blinking my tears away, I push myself up and wonder how Liam will react. That I have a son, and my mum is alive. Will he be jealous?

"Once Erin and Nicky have finished their tasks of deactivating the magical traps, they'll retrieve and remove the spells on your mum," Melody states. "Though I would advise waiting a few days until you try and obtain Ian. It will be hard to convince Sabrina to hand him over to you. Although there is a spell you can use; it would forcefully grant her the ability to see the supernatural and allow you to explain why it is best that Ian goes with you."

"Okay," I say. I'm exhausted, too tired to do this anymore. "You'll be leaving, I assume soon?"

"Yes," Melody confirms. "More people need saving. I won't be alone. Cathy and Theon will accompany me."

"I thought Cathy was in a coma?"

"She'll wake in a few hours. Then tomorrow, we will be gone."

"No offence, well, some offence—I hope we never meet again."

"We will meet again," Melody retorts stiffly. "I don't know when, nevertheless we will meet one way or another. Our fates are interconnected. I will send a few people your way. I know you are interested in helping those who need it."

I nod my head in agreement. I'll help anyone who needs it, like Melody did for me. There are no more words to be spoken between us.

Melody will be gone tomorrow with Theon and Cathy, while her brother, Dylan, will be taking his family to Jared's ancestral pack in California. I overheard their conversation. I think a lot of refugees are departing tomorrow, although some will remain so they can join Willow pack. And I'll protect them, so that an attack, like we had today, never happens again.

I've rested and had two blood bags. Liam is busy doing paperwork at his desk. He's wearing a purple tee and black distressed jeans. The bed is comfortable, very different to the concrete I had slept on some days prior, in that abandoned warehouse.

I have a book open on my lap, where the incantation I'll perform on Sabrina stares back at me. It is late evening, Erin and Nicky haven't returned with Mum. Part of me can't believe it's true, that Mum is alive and I have a son.

Liam handled the news well, although there was a jolt of jealousy in the soul bond when I mentioned my mum was alive. And when I mentioned my ex, there was another jolt. Though I could feel he was looking forward to meeting Ian—my son. It sounds ridiculous that I have a son. I'm eighteen and committed patricide today. Only to find out I have a son. It kind of makes it seem like the universe has a sense of humour.

What type of father will I be? Will I be a terrible one? Will my kid hate me? *Probably will,* I muse, *I'm going to take him from the sole family he knows.* I could leave him there, but there could be a chance some supernatural bigot will stumble upon my boy and murder him!

No, I can't take that chance. Nor will Sabrina, when she understands. A tiny part of me wonders if she broke up with me because she found out she was pregnant. Her parents were quite religious, they might have sent her away to her grandparents during the pregnancy. In fact, she might have been sent away right after breaking up with me, as I didn't see her around Oxstead once we broke up, and the town isn't exactly big.

Flicking my wrist, the book on my lap closes and soars onto one of shelves on the bookcases. Liam glances at me, and my heart aches. I don't think I will ever forgive Melody; she lied about Mum being dead, didn't tell me about my blood-purist Aunt, and failed to inform me of my son—Ian Green.

I think the last one hurts the most. My son doesn't know me. I haven't been there for him. I grew up without a father. It hurt, and I was jealous of everyone for having one. Then that jealousy turned to bitterness when I learned my father wanted to kill me!

I flinch as Liam touches me, kneeling in front of me. A concerned look on his face. "What's wrong Clay?"

"I don't know how to be a father, and I've missed a lot already. Not to mention, I'm going to have to take him away from his mother and grandparents."

"Because they can't protect him. And it's not like you're going to forbid them to ever see Ian again. They can visit."

"I know that, I just loathe how hybrids are hated," I state bitterly. "How can I raise him in this world? I can't kill every bigot?"

"There will always be those who think they are better than others. All we can do is raise him to know that he isn't a monster or an abomination."

I nod, my thoughts take me away. I haven't even met my boy, and the idea of people thinking of him as an abomination confuses me and makes me sick to my core. I finally understand—I understand why Mum chose me over her soulmate. This emotion towards Ian is different, primitive and animalistic.

I don't think I could pick between Liam and Ian. Unless Liam desired harm on Ian. Then I would flee with Ian to protect him.

There is no other option, the child needs protection. I allow myself to cry. I hadn't cried at the nexus-point, I didn't allow myself. I do now, crying in happiness that Mum is alive, crying for the loss of time with my son, and crying for the unfairness of this world.

"I'm here," my Alpha-boy mumbles, bringing my sobbing form onto the floor with him, hugging me tight to his body with his strong manly arms. "So much has happened today."

"So much has happened in eight days," I choke out between my sobs.

Liam hums in agreement, rocking me. Sleep tugs at my consciousness, and I'm powerless to resist. I descend into oblivion. It doesn't last long as I awaken to the sensation of someone stroking my hair. Peeling my eyelids, a crack, I see a woman thought long dead— Mum. Her hair has gone grey in my absence, her face is more wrinkled, though her eyes are as vibrant as ever. Mum's sister, the bitch, was an uglier version of her.

I want to tell Mum everything, and I want her to meet Liam too. If she hated him, I would die. I wiggle a tiny bit, to get more comfortable on the bed.

Laughing softly, her hand becomes limp in my hair, a small smile spreading onto her beautiful face. "I know you're awake, my sweet boy."

"I m-missed y-you so m-much," I stutter opening my burning eyes wide. Mum gasps and stares into my blazing golden eyes. "They're gorgeous."

I blush and the burning sensation fades, causing my eyes to revert to their original form. "However, classics are always better."

Blushing again, I sit up and hug her, burying my face into the crook of her neck. Her scent is unchanged. It's like I'm a child again. Her arms wrap around me delicately, and she begins to sing a song she used to sing at bedtime. The tears come again, and I let them fall. She's here, my mum is here, and she is alive. I pray to the Goddess and all other deities that this is not a dream.

CHAPTER XXIX

After pulling away from our hug, I rest my head in Mum's lap, her fingers sliding through my hair again. It doesn't seem like reality that Mum is here. That she's alive and touching me. That we can spend time together again.

"Liam is a lovely young man," Mum comments, and I blush harder than ever. "Seems like a real nice guy. He said he was going to welcome people into his pack when he left. Though not before he welcomed me to his and your pack," she smiles fondly. "Not that he could make me go."

"You promise," I plead childishly.

"I promise. So, tell me what happened. The stench of burning flesh is prolific outside. That needs explaining."

Nervously, I tell her about everything that has happened. About living life on the streets, about meeting Melody and the events that followed. I spoke in such detail, I felt as if I was there again, and by the time I explain what happened today, Mum is whiter than a sheet. Still, she waits patiently for me to tell her everything.

"Okay, let me get this right. My sister tried to kill you, and my suspicion that she did kill Logan was correct. Thomas is dead, you killed him too. You have a son with that Sabrina girl called Ian. And, for whatever reason, you didn't feel comfortable telling me you were bi?"

"Never found the right moment."

"I wouldn't have cared. You're my world."

"I know that now! I understand. I haven't even met Ian and I understand."

"I'm glad you understand." She sighs in the only way mothers can. "Though, I can't believe I am a forty-three-year-old grandma."

"There have been younger ones."

She chuckles. "You're right there."

I smile. "This can't be real, you being here."

"It is real, I would be able to tell if it wasn't," Mum states bitterly. "As these last years have felt like a dream. My body wasn't my own. Controlled by something else. By the spells he had me under. My reality was a horrific nightmare." Pausing, she steadies herself. "His coming home was the worst—I would be the dutiful wife." She shivers in disgust. "I will always remember screaming internally, as my body did whatever he wanted. I had no power."

"There are no words," I snarl. "I wish I could kill him again."

"Me too, me too, my sweet boy. I just pray he will never return."

"He won't. He is gone. I made sure of that. He won't be returning —ever."

Tears twinkle in her eyes, and I discover that my hatred for the person society would call my father somehow grows deeper. Sitting up, I hug Mum, hoping my embrace will sooth her anguish. She sobs and a growl escapes my lips, a proper guttural growl. Parting, I kiss her forehead. "I love you, Mum."

"I love you, my sweet boy." She smiles weakly as I wipe her tears away. "Always."

I do not have time to say anything else as Liam enters. I'm conflicted. Unsure if I should leave Mum or go to Liam. Mum makes the choice for me. She waves me away, in dismissive fashion. "I'm okay."

Nodding, I get off the bed and walk up to Liam. Mum's smile seems to warm. I quickly peck Liam on the lips and step back, noticing his cheeks tinge red at the brief display of affection. I had missed him, despite being in the company of my long-lost mother.

"No need to be embarrassed dear," Mum says kindly, hopping off the bed and approaching us—she had been addressing Liam's blush. "You are both grownups, engaged and soulmates. I'm not a prude. I'm going to find a room now. I look forward to spending time with you, Liam."

"Me?" Liam replies, dumbstruck.

"Of course, you're going to be my son-in-law. You can call me Mum if you want, or Maria if that's more comfortable."

Alpha-boy flushes a darker red. "I think Maria to start off, if that's okay?"

"That's perfectly fine, dear." Liam stiffens as Mum hugs him. It isn't a long embrace, a few seconds max. Nevertheless, I see he is shaken by it. I don't think he or I ever expected to get Mum-hugs again.

Once releasing him, Mum spins on her heels and walks out the door, shutting it, silently behind her. My heart aches seeing her leave, though I know I will see her again. That it won't be the last time. That we'll have plenty of time.

CHAPTER XXX

"Your Mum is very friendly," Liam comments, smiling subduedly as I wrap my arms around his neck.

"She always has been." I smile, pecking another quick kiss on Liam's lips. "I can't believe she is here," I pause. "Or that I have a son." Pausing again, I nervously bite my lower lip. "I'm scared this might be a dream. That I'll wake up."

"This isn't a dream." He kisses me roughly, pushing my arms away from his neck and pinning my wrist against the wall above my head. "This is life. Our life."

His rough kiss has brought my quick pecks to shame.

"I love you," I proclaim, my body electrified and energised. "I'll always love you."

He smiles smugly, his lips pressing kisses to my neck and jaw. Excitement and trepidation wiggle inside me. The danger has passed. We are free. We are predators. We are the winners. Liam releases my hands, kissing me lovingly on the lips. My heart flutters painfully fast. Carefully, he tugs his hoodie off my body, letting it drift onto the floor.

"Tomorrow," Liam whispers against my lips, "we can finally go on our run."

"We can," I chuckle. "We finally can."

"I'll outrun you in my wolf form."

"Don't count on it, Alpha-boy."

"Fuck, I love it when you call me that." His hot lips crush against mine—dominant and passionate. His calloused hands rip the tee right off me, and I do the same to his. Our naked torsos pressing against one another.

His mouth withdraws from mine, pressing kisses lower and lower. On my throat. On my chest. On my navel. And back up, until our lips are reunited.

His fingers clumsily try to pull my jog bottoms down, while my hands nimbly unbutton his jean. Cold air greets my legs as my jog bottoms plummet to the floor. Stepping out of them, Liam does the same. For the first time, we're both in our underwear together. My heart beats faster than should be possible.

"Are we going to do this?" I say between kisses, our soul bond consumed with lust. Liam mumbles in confirmation, and I gasp as he throws me onto the bed. A slight nervousness fills me. This will be the first time we'll be together, and my first with a man. Plus, I doubt Liam will be on the bottom. Not that it worries me. I know the spell to make me ready to receive him. And I'm kind of curious to know what it is like.

Then abruptly, Liam dives on top of me and starts grinding his arse on my manhood, gifting me waves of pleasure. Any thoughts or nervousness are gone in an instant. And that's before his fingers start to tweak my rock-hard nipples.

"My Alpha-boy," I moan out, my senses distorted, and Liam is the single entity in my universe. He always will be.

"My Clay," Liam moans back.

I flip our positions and break our kiss, my body thrumming and tingling with pure lust. My hands run the length of Liam's naked torso, as I grind against Liam's manhood. Our underwear is in the way. They need to be removed. I need to be with him. I need to know him.

Rolling off my Alpha-boy, I mumble an incantation, causing my insides to tingle, and I'm prepared. I give him a nod, indicating I'm ready. He smiles and moves over to me, his right hand dragging my underwear to my ankles, causing my whole body to tremble.

Then seductively and annoyingly, he slowly and teasingly lowers his boxers. And oh boy, am I pleased with what I see. Tegan, you have no idea how right you were...

Soon, my eyes are screwed shut, as I am lost to the sensation of his touch, his kisses and his great manhood. My world trembles, pleasure clouding my mind. Is this what my venom is like? Liam mumbles continuously that he loves me. I reply with a string of moans and declarations of dedication, in clumsy unfiltered words. I've wanted this since we met. Every kiss, every touch, every 'I love you' has led to this. We will be together forever. Or until he dies.

Liam bites my bottom lip; I gasp into the kiss. Our moans vibrate as we make-out. His calloused hands endlessly rove up and down my body, never settling for long, while my own hands do the same to him. It is almost like, if we weren't to touch each other, in all the ways we could, we would die—maybe we would, who knows.

Then suddenly, my eyes fly open and everything goes white, as we convulse and scream in orgasmic pleasure.

For a few minutes afterwards, we just lay there breathing. Connected in a way, neither of us will ever be with someone else again.

Eventually, we withdraw and untangle from each other, our bodies sweaty and spent. Snuggling up against one another, sleep and exhaustion weighs us down. Liam kisses my forehead. I want this every day, to be together, happy and safe.

"That was a great experience," Liam croaks sleepily.

"Next time," I mumble, "we should go slower. We rushed."

"We did," he agrees, sleep claiming him pretty much instantly, a snore billowing out of his talented mouth. Rolling my eyes, I allow sleep to carry me away too, our soul bond singing in unity. I'll always remember this day, for the joys and horrors—it was an eventful day. A day that will haunt my dreams and nightmares.

CHAPTER XXXI

Erin and Nicky were the first to go in the morning. It was vaguely warm, a stark contrast to the frigid temperature of yesterday. The two of them took Cordelia with them, no one objected. The babe is happiest when she is among the Parry siblings. Erin and Nicky both agreed if we ever needed help, to give them a shout, and I offered the same to them. I would miss them calling me 'wee one'.

Nicky reminded me to be careful of the Grand Coven, and that they may come for me one day. Then, Erin and I decided to keep in contact through email. We hadn't reached the friendship level, but we would in time.

Dylan, Jared and Katie were next to go. Dylan was in obvious mourning for Ashley, his mother. Jared hugged me and wished me the best of luck. Katie nodded shyly at me as her goodbye. A few groups of refugees left after them, the little plump boy I had saved and his parents were among them.

Then, Melody, Theon and a battered Cathy were next. I was surprised to see that Cathy's right leg ended in a stump. The leg ended just below her kneecap; thus, she leaned heavily on a crutch. She was pale, with dark circles under her eyes, and no longer like the angry woman I first met, or the woman who had tried to soothe my guilt. It seemed that Cathy had lost her spark.

Theon looked exhausted, and had equally dark circles under his eyes, keeping an arm around Melody's shoulder as if he feared she would vanish.

Melody appeared unaffected by the loss of life, or her mother's death—something that I believe might have caused a rift between her and Dylan. She rationalised her decisions again with me, and reaffirmed she would send those in need, so I can help them. Melody also gave me a number if I ever wanted to contact her. I doubt I will. It was a bitter end to our friendship, or was it ever a friendship? Hard to tell. Still, I owe her. Melody put me on the path that led me here, that brought me to my Alpha-boy.

No one else departed after them. The remaining refugees were absorbed into Willow pack, the ones that hadn't already done it last night, that is. Liam then went to the training ground to lead combat drills. It was Tegan's first, and she looked so alive and free as she sparred, though it was creepy to see her eerie empty blank eyes surveying her attackers.

Mum watched the combat training with me, and we talked in low whispers, reminiscing about our memories in Oxstead. Although she couldn't stay that long, needing to return to bed, as her body hasn't fully recovered from being freed of the spells she had been under.

In all, the day so far has been rather boring. Liam is finishing up a few mundane tasks at his desk, so we can head out on our run. I'm wearing a lilac-coloured tee, jog bottoms and my trusty combat boots. Liam is in a similar attire, jog bottoms, trainers and a sweatshirt.

I will always treasure last night.

When we woke up this morning, before we went out and did the goodbyes, I had my morning feed and we fooled around a bit, doing things that we had left out in the rush of our first time. Then we thoroughly brushed our teeth, showered together and fooled around again. Forcing us to brush our teeth and shower again. Liam's body, like mine to him, is now a well-known canvas, our bodies holding no secrets from one another.

"I'm going outside while you finish up," I state. Alpha-boy gives me a distracted nod as he sorts through papers and simultaneously types on his laptop.

Outside, it's humid. Kids play games, adults lie about on blankets, and teenagers hide in the shadows with their phones.

Tegan catches my eye from the porch, wearing a tank top, flip-flops and shorts. Her chocolate brown eyes are watching some kids wistfully. She doesn't notice me standing next to her right away. When she does, she flinches, placing her hand over her heart.

"Goddess, you scared me." Tegan laughs tensely. "Someone should put a bell on you."

"Maybe they did," I deadpan.

Tegan snorts. "I doubt it. So, what brings you to me?"

"We haven't talked. I wanted to see how you're doing."

"I'm great, I'm a werewolf," her irises and pupils vanish, her eerie blank eyes gazing into my soul. "All thanks to Melody and you."

"You could have died? Right?"

"Yes, and it's what I wanted. Not dying, but being a werewolf. It took me an hour or two to decide though. It was a very agonising experience, worse than the time with Victor."

I hum noncommittally. "It was a reckless decision; I don't want to lose you. You're my single friend here."

"Really?" Tegan frowns in surprise.

"It's not like I've been talking to anyone else."

"I guess not."

"Now, tell me, was there another cost, other than possibly dying?"

Tegan sits down. I copy her decision, observing as her pupil and iris return to both her eyes. Tegan's gaze locks onto the children once more. "Melody said if I agreed to the bite, I could die. And, if I survived, my likelihood of conceiving a child is low. I know you have a son. Secrets and gossip and all that in a pack. My point being, I know you're a parent and I know JJ wants children. However, I have not wanted them until this moment—now that I might not be able to." A sole tear streams down her cheek. "It wasn't easy seeing the supernatural growing up. To this day, my parents and relatives think I'm a liar, or mentally ill or both. So, the idea of having children, and them possibly being like me, horrified me. However, if I had children now, they would be normal werewolves."

"They wouldn't be a hybrid and different, like me, like my son."

"No, I hope—I didn't mean to, I'm not—"

"I know you're not," I interject. "Being a hybrid is hard. My son will have a hard life because he inherited my impure blood." We descend into stifling silence. My guilt towards my son is unbearable. Tomorrow, I will see him, and explain to Sabrina and her parents why Ian must be with me. I will be unable to wait any longer. Dismissing my problems, I think about Tegan's. "I can't make any promises, but I could help you get pregnant."

Her eyebrows rise basically to her hairline. "Did you just say you would help me get pregnant?"

"Ew, not physically. No offence—I would've totally been interested once. Although, I'm happily soul bonded and engaged now."

"I heard," Tegan says, taking my hand and examining the engagement ring. "It's pretty. So, how could you aid me in my desire to be pregnant? If not physically."

"A fertility potion. It's how I was conceived, as vampires are sterile, because they are undead beings."

"Do you think you could brew one?"

"In time. Give me a few months, and it'll allow you to decide if you want to be pregnant or not."

"You are a great friend, Clay."

"And you are too."

She smiles and places her head on my shoulder. Tegan may no longer be an outcast, yet she will always remember, and thus, she will not distance herself from me. Pressing a chaste kiss to her forehead, I am content to sit here. Melody may not have been a true friend, but Tegan is.

"You know," I begin, "you once asked me if I had seen Liam's dick, and I have now. I know it very well." Moving my hands apart, I give a rough estimation of my Alpha-boy's manhood.

Tegan whistles. "How are you walking?"

"Hybrid healing and magic."

"I am j-e-a-l-o-u-s, 'cause I'm still a bit sore from last night's celebration, and I have the benefit of werewolf healing." She waggles her eyebrows, and I chuckle. "Anyway, I'll always remember my first time with JJ—his inexperience was evident then. Was yours memorable?"

"Yep, though we didn't do much foreplay and it was rather frenzied. I'm pleased that I memorised that incantation I used to prepare myself for him. I wanted him desperately; I didn't really have time to stop. And the spell is better and faster."

"Too much information," Tegan says with a laugh. "And I recall that feeling. It doesn't ever go away." she pauses. "Just so you know, many pack members are probably eavesdropping."

"Secrets and gossip and whatnot, right? Plus, I don't really care. You?"

"Nope, you heard that, your Alpha-Male and Beta-Female, don't fucking care if you listen?" Several pack members, who obviously had been listening, abruptly begin talking to whoever is near them, embarrassed to be caught or accused of listening. "Boo, a bunch of cowards. How can the lot of them face what we did yesterday, but be shamed they were caught eavesdropping?"

I shrug. "Social convention?"

Tegan hums in response and gasps as JJ plops down next to her and kisses her passionately. When they withdraw, they begin to talk in hushed tones. Fortunately, Liam exits the log cabin at that moment, and I know it is time for our run. Muttering a goodbye, I hurry to Liam's side, ignoring their looks, stares and mumbling. They don't matter in that moment; what matters is my Liam.

We kiss, his hands sinfully cupping and squeezing my bottom. My arms hug his neck, as his teeth bite my bottom lip, eliciting a moan. Part of me wants to drag Liam into our little log cabin and make love, until the sun sets and rises again. Although we don't. The two of us part and hold hands. Strolling towards the nexus-point. The place we decided to start our run. Later, I would recall that those who witnessed our passionate making out were smiling happily in our direction, pleased to see their Alpha and Alpha-Male so deeply in love.

CHAPTER XXXII

I stretch, preparing to run, while Liam discards his clothing. His nudity fills me with dirty thoughts and pleasurable memories. He keeps his engagement ring on, and I know it has an enchantment that stops it from being destroyed if Liam shifts. As he begins his transformation, I can't defend myself from feeling a spark of jealousy. I will not know that. Never know what it's like.

Shaking my head, I focus on Alpha-boy. His hulking wolf form trots towards me and licks my face. Exclaiming in disgust, I grin. Our soul bond is stronger than it was, now that we've made love, and I can almost sense his thoughts.

As we spend more time together, feel deeper for one another, our soul bond will only grow. With our soul bond stronger, I realise that I could only sense his emotions when we were in close proximity. Though that isn't how it is anymore. I felt him the entire time I chatted to Tegan, and while he led combat training.

Patting Liam's nose, he nods and gives me a wolfish smile, his big tongue lolling out of his mouth. Smiling, I kiss his forehead, stroking the fur on the side of his neck. Eyes burning, we get into our running positions. Quiet descends around us until the moment we speed forward, as if the forest has been waiting, holding its breath.

I keep pace, easily evading and leaping over any obstacle. The rush of wind and blurriness of my surroundings is dizzying. Liam increases his speed, smirking somehow. I push myself harder, managing to move in front of him. Growling, he pounces over me, a flurry of mud splashing me.

"A dirty trick," I shout.

Liam's response is chortling, a peculiar sound to hear from a wolf. Using my magic, it helps propel me faster, making my surroundings a blur of colour. The single in-focus constant is the cheat in front of me. I overtake him, his wolfish chortle replaced with a playful growl.

Taking a sharp left, I pivot, leap into the air and push against a tree trunk. Causing the unfortunate tree to split in two as I fling myself faster than a bullet, way ahead of Alpha-boy. He makes an indigent whine, as I land running, *eat my dust loser*. However, that thought is promptly forgotten, the moment I trip and topple head first into a lake. The murky water softens the blow, although it is jarring, resulting in a few seconds of momentary paralysis.

Swimming to the surface, I am greeted by the sight of Liam the wolf, on his back whimpering, chortling and huffing in apparent hysterics. Crossing my arms, I pout, kicking my legs to keep me afloat. The memories of how I learnt to swim meet my mind. It was one of Mum's possibly bad parenting moves. She pushed me into the deep end, at age three, with no idea how to swim. The lifeguard had to intervene. Next week, she did the same and the next, until I figured it out. Dismissing the memories, I ask Liam sarcastically, "Want to see something funny?"

He doesn't hear and continues his hysterics. I decide to follow through with my idea. Focusing on him, I imagine what I want to happen. A second later, Liam flies head first into the lake's murky water, making me chuckle. When he surfaces, my chuckling becomes howls of laughter.

Liam's fur clings to him. His paws propelling him afloat, he looks like a big wet dog, save for his luminous red eyes.

His revenge is a lick to my face. Exclaiming in disgust again, I wrap my arms around his neck. He goes limp, his big head resting on my shoulder, leaving me all the work to keep us afloat. The forest goes quiet again, and surprise bubbles inside me. A part of me, I've not noticed, feels complete having run through the forest with Liam. It is like that piece of me was asleep, waiting for this moment.

Unexpectedly, our soul bond goes taunt and pulsates. A sharp pain rockets down my spine. My eyesight vanishes, as does my grip on Liam. The world disappears. I am alone in darkness.

Breathe through the pain. I listen to Liam's voice, and the pain lessens. *You can do this.* Light returns. The world reforms. I'm on the bank of the lake. Liam is above me, tongue dangling out of his mouth. His wide, loving red eyes looking down on me. *You're beautiful.* I can hear his voice in my mind. *You can,* Liam confirms.

I stand, my paws struggling—wait paws? Lifting one up, I examine the caramel furred paw. Tilting my head to the side, my ears twitch. Everything is louder and sharper. Turning in a circle, I chase my tail—a weird useless appendage that I cannot control. Pausing, my nose twitches, the scent of prey is close. Wait, I don't need meat. This is instinct. Shaking my head, I sit on my haunches, the annoying tail flicking.

I have a wolf form—glancing at the lake's water, I see my reflection. I'm a wolf of equal size to Liam, completely caramel coloured, with blazing golden eyes. Licking my chops, Liam rubs his snout against my throat. My heart whines as I whimper. I have a wolf form, I'm immortal, and I have magic. I'm all the best parts of the three species, four if you count humans and their best quality: humanity.

Nuzzling against Liam, we share thoughts, memories and long mental conversations, as well as Alpha-boy teaching me how to shield my mind from him. Apparently, most soulmates dislike hearing their partner's thoughts, considering it an invasion of privacy. I can understand that. However, I wish to be as open as possible.

I will hold no secrets; I whisper into Liam's mind.

Nor I, he agrees and we continue sharing thoughts and memories. The day passes, but we don't notice. All that existed in the world, in those moments—was us.

CHAPTER XXXIII

It is late evening when we return to the nexus-point, having spent most of the day lazing on the lakeside. We are closer than I ever thought possible—my memories live inside him, and his memories live inside me. The knowledge of his brothers and parents swirl within me. They were amazing people, and I am pleased to know them, even if they are second-hand experiences.

Liam shifts back into his human form, then puts his underwear on, before coaching me, in how to shift back. The process is agony, but I don't lose consciousness this time, and unlike Tegan, I don't faint once returning to my human form.

Standing, he helps me pull on his jog bottom, as my own clothing was reduced to shreds. The clothing can be replaced. Though I am saddened the combat boots were destroyed, I had grown to like them.

"Today, by my standards, was rather mundane," Liam says, gripping my chin between his fingers. "If every day is like this, I will not know dissatisfaction."

"I could never be dissatisfied by you."

He grins. "I love you, Clay, my special, amazing mate."

I flush and kiss him. I'm not an abomination. I'm special and different, and that doesn't always mean wrong. And I believe it. If I didn't, I would need to—how else could I raise my son to be proud of who he is? Mum tried, she failed, it is not her fault. Only another hybrid can understand the duality, confusion and hate. Knowing that people hated me simply for existing made me hate myself. How couldn't I? My own Father could not love me. Ian will not know that. He'll know unconditional love. No matter what.

One day, Ian could be like me with a wolf form, immortality and magic. Though it seems selfish of me, to wish that he is immortal? I banish that thought out of my mind, and regrettably, I know I will contact Melody. I won't ever trust her again, yet she can be a useful source of information. I'll just have to take everything she says with a grain of salt. For I have to know if Ian is immortal.

I groan into the kiss as Liam slams me against a tree, the bark scratching my skin harshly. He tweaks my already hard nipples, and my breath escapes in frantic gasps. The wolf inside me, which is the presence of my animalistic instincts, surges, yearning to be bred by its mate.

My claws dig through Liam's shoulder blades. Half of me wants to run away, because I've made him bleed. Except, this new side of me whispers and encourages me to be rougher. He's an Alpha, he can take rough treatment. Clamping down on his bottom lip, Liam moans. His sweet blood dribbles into my thirsty mouth. Maybe my venom has slipped into his bloodstream. No, if that was the case, he would be under my control.

Liam fails to pull down the jog bottom he helped me into. Rolling my eyes, I shove him away, yank them down, step out of them and dive at him. Knocking us both roughly onto the hard ground.

Kissing him, my arms tangle about him in a fierce embrace, as he frantically rips his underwear off so we can grind our naked bodies together.

The notion of returning to the clearing in modesty is gone. It's not like nudity is frowned upon. Hell, I've seen Tegan naked when she shifted back. Huh, I guess then, it should have been awkward when we talked earlier. Not to mention everyone has seen Liam nude already.

"I love you, Clay," Liam moans between kisses. "I'll love you until I die."

My heart shatters and I roll off him. Shakily, I stand, Liam does too, a look of confusion on his face. He tries to come close to me. I step away and hug myself, steadying my heart. "You will not die—I will not allow it." I take a shuddering breath, hearing him say he would die, just now, it hurt worse than anything. "How I could stomach the idea of you dying is impossible for me to comprehend. How could I? My heart is in shards at the thought of you dead." Pausing, I compel my maelstrom of emotions to calm, as I drop my arms to my side. "I told you that I would move heaven and earth, and that I would accomplish it. And I know I would. No one will step in my way, not fate or death or the Goddess. For I will never let you die." I ball my clawed hands, watching coolly as they explode into silver flames. "I am among the strongest beings in history. I don't say that with arrogance, I state it as a fact. I am faster and stronger than any being I have encountered. I am immortal, I can shift into a wolf and I have magic. I may be inexperienced, but in years or months' time, I will master it," the silver flames dissipate. "Nothing will ever stand in my way. If I wished, I know I could bring great anguish and doom to this world. What Thomas, Victor and Henri did would look like a child's tantrum by comparison. Do you fear me, Liam? I could become the wild cruel killing-obsessed beast that you heard stories of. All it would take is one action, to drive me to the brink—your death." My mind rebels at the thought of him dying, it is something I will not let happen, even if it's old age. "I love my mum and I love my son, despite having not met him. But if you were to die, I do not hold the strength Alpha Andrew, Ashley or Theon possessed to continue going without their other half. If you die—I die with you."

Liam is gaping at me, jaw hanging wide open. I'm a little surprised, I had reassured myself that we would have years and decades. Though, I know now, having spent a practically perfect carefree day with him, no matter how much time I spend with my Alpha-boy, it will not be enough. The idea of him dying destroys me. My wolf and magic scream in fury. Nothing will ever separate us.

Regaining his composure, Liam steps towards me and lifts me into his arms, my legs wrapping around his waist. "I will not fear you and I will not die. We will figure out a way," he promises. "And you will never become a wild cruel killing-obsessed beast. I regret ever speaking those words. Forgive me."

"You could rip my heart out, and I would forgive you."

"I wish I could ask you to marry me again."

"Then we would ask that question every day."

He chuckles and poses a question I would gladly hear until eternity. "Marry me?"

"Yes," I reply. "And my answer will be the same, the next day and the next, and in centuries time, I will still be saying yes."

"Then is shall be the favourite part of my day," he states happily, before frowning. "I know if we did not have this soul bond that we may have—"

"Shut up," I interject angrily. "I would always choose you, in this life and every life. Liam, you are my true love."

Tears glimmer in his red eyes. "Clay, you've lived up to every expectation I've ever had of a mate. I thought that impossible."

"Not impossible, improbable, that I would live up to your expectation."

"So, fucking confident."

"I know I am, Alpha-boy."

Liam shivers, no words escape either of us, we are true loves, soulmates and fiancés. Nothing will ever get between us— nothing. And if someone or something tries, oh boy, they'll be in trouble.

I kiss him, our soul bond a tsunami of emotion. My mind and his, open to each other, memories glossed with lust and love recycled between us. My heart swells in blissful agony.

Death, fate and the Goddess, beware, if you dare claim Liam Willow, the formidable force of Clay Darby will be brought upon you.

Liam lies down, I follow, mumbling the incantation that makes my inside tingles. Soon, our bodies move in sync. The world vanishes again. Liam is my sun, my stars, my planets and my universe. Other people are my moons. Liam, though, will eternally be my sun, my stars and my planets.

You are everything to me too, Liam confesses, the words echoing forever in my mind.

Our love will be an everlasting inferno, I retort. Liam howls and I throw my head back, releasing my own howl as I stare up at the night sky.

The full moon hangs low among glittering stars, basking us in moonlight. Perspiration drips down our bodies, and the nexus-point below us undulates, pulsating and twitching due to my intense emotions.

Strangely, my veins begin illuminating a shimmering molten gold as I approach orgasmic rapture. Arching my back, bolts of electricity blast out of my palms, and my inner wolf howls in ecstasy. Thank the Goddess, my hands have been directed upwards. Bending down, I snog Liam, my heart beating in union with his—we are one.

Collapsing next to my Alpha-boy, I am spent and exhaustion barrels down onto me. Liam's hooded red eyes lock with mine, memories and emotions are conveyed silently between us. He is mine, and I am his. Dare to claim him, and you'll find yourself facing me. For a split second, I swear that an ancient feminine voice whispers, *I wouldn't dare, young immortal, I wouldn't dare.* Followed by a musical laugh.

Shaking my head, I dwell on my life. I can't believe at one point; I despised my impure blood, that I resented it. Without it, I could not hope to spend an eternity with my true love, or possibly my son. Turning onto my side, I embrace Alpha-boy under the night sky, our hearts and soul bond a maelstrom of happiness, as we descend into a peaceful, loving, happy oblivion. Thank you, Goddess, for my life, my Alpha-boy and my impure blood—thank you...

THE END

ACKNOWLEDGMENTS

Wow! I finished it! This is the first story I ever properly finished. It might not be a masterpiece, but I did it. Especially, when I did it with a chronic illness. Who can say that?

I didn't think it would be possible or to be able to self-publish. However, I've done it and it wouldn't have happened, without the help and encouragement of my biggest fan, carer and parent – my mum. She has always been there for me, be it taking me to medical appointments or listening to how I'm feeling or trying to help me, in figuring out how to self-publish. Thank you, Mum.

Additionally, I would like to thank my tutors, all of whom had a hand in moulding me into the writer I am today. Though, most of my improvements have been, by just writing madly and reading anything. Lastly, I would like to thank the ever-helpful Gareth Clegg who edited, did the layout and made my marvellous cover.

Also, a special thank you to anyone who spent their time reading this tale of acceptance.

P.S. It would be most appreciated if you left a review, every review can help someone else discover my book. I really want to be able to continue my author journey, as being an author is my goal in life. And if you don't, no hard feelings, just having read my book means the world to me.

AUTHOR BIO

Oliver Iredale is a fledgling British author and sufferer of myalgic encephalomyelitis (M.E). When he can't be found resting or reading or watching tv shows (normally fantasy or horror of origin), he can be discovered writing. Lost in his make-believe worlds, normally in company of his cat. His goal in life is to be a full-time, professional author. Something he only recently tried to accomplish, after being inspired by a fellow writer.

Printed in Great Britain
by Amazon

49912002R00118